Also by Edward Wilson

Cicatrix, A Novel

The Sibyl's Mistake

A Novel

Edward Wilson

iUniverse, Inc.

New York   Bloomington

The Sibyl's Mistake
A Novel

iUniverse books may be ordered through booksellers or by contacting:

iUniverse
1663 Liberty Drive
Bloomington, IN 47403
www.iuniverse.com
1-800-Authors (1-800-288-4677)

Because of the dynamic nature of the Internet, any Web addresses or links contained in this book may have changed since publication and may no longer be valid. The views expressed in this work are solely those of the author and do not necessarily reflect the views of the publisher, and the publisher hereby disclaims any responsibility for them.

ISBN: 978-1-4502-5030-6 (sc)
ISBN: 978-1-4502-5027-6 (ebook)
ISBN: 978-1-4502-5031-3 (dj)

Library of Congress Control Number: 2010911832

Printed in the United States of America

iUniverse rev. date: 9/14/2010

For Giovanni Battista Solferino
who showed me his Naples.

CONTENTS

INTRODUCTION

The Sibyl's Mistake is a Mediterranean novel, the Mediterranean of Homer and Virgil, of Petronius and Suetonius, of Dante and Milton, of Casanova and Corvo, of Shelley and Goethe, of Forster and Cavafy, of Douglas and Durrell, of Hazzard and Sontag, of Hoffstader and Beard. It was during a period when I was in thrall to Naples that the germ of the present work formed and I began to hope that I myself might add another volume to the works of this august company. I wrote night after night as the story poured out of my mind and into my computer. One sunrise, it was completed. My hope is that readers will delight in the adventures of our fellow travelers in the following pages.

1. ARRIVALS

Traffic noises came up from the street below, and a light wind blew in from the Mediterranean. In the near distance, shipping on the bay was very active in the morning sunlight, streaking its surface with the wakes of arriving and departing freighters, cruise ships, and ferries that ran to other mainland ports and some islands. Above the bay, Vesuvius loomed high on the left and below it the shoreline curved away to the right in a parabola that ended with the Sorrentine Peninsula tip and then lined up again at Capri, an offshore continuation on a submerged ridge. The sweep of Siren Land.

Frank Bones paused briefly to admire the view from the window and again felt very pleased with himself to be in Naples. He put a last reprint box on the bookshelf and then took a break from unpacking his research library. Today officially was the first day of his sabbatical year from the university at Berkeley. Last week, he had come in on the long but uneventful flight from San Francisco to move into his new condo. The household goods and books that he had boxed and shipped finally had arrived, late but intact, and were nearly installed.

Less than a year ago, Bones had been on his beloved motorcycle on a pursuit from California down the Baja California peninsula on what he considered to be a mission of justice to redress a personal physical injury deliberately inflicted on him as an act of domination by a previously trusted young man. His long association with the Code of the San Francisco-based gay, sado-masochistic, motorcycle gang named the Blackguards, to which they both belonged, required such action, especially since he had been the mentor of the perpetrator who was seeking membership. The ultimate indignity was that the younger man had proposed to demonstrate his worthiness for membership by unexpectedly overpowering Bones, his nominal master.

When that matter was settled in Mexico to his satisfaction, Bones resigned from the Blackguards, partly because his years of membership had dulled his original enthusiasm to quiet boredom with the entire group, especially the rigid regimentation which attended everything. Bones wanted a new life.

He already had a tenured professorship at the University of California at Berkeley and a strong intellectual interest in his special field, fossil plants. This, combined with a fascination for the geologic history of the Campania area of Italy, in which Naples is located, and an understanding of its great research potential because its fossil plant record was so exquisitely preserved, led him to decide to transfer to the University of Naples in order to make the study of this flora the research project of the remainder of his career. He was a good field man and a well-known researcher, spoke and read Italian fluently, and had little difficulty acquiring a one-year Visiting Professorship with teaching and publishing responsibilities. He hoped to be able to turn this into a permanent position—difficult, he knew, but not impossible.

His age - middle forties - would permit him potential time to accomplish these goals and free him from the relatively insubstantial competition of younger academics, both important to any committees considering him for employment at the University of Naples. He also anticipated the possibility - even the likelihood - of the arrival in Naples of his younger Blackguard former colleague, especially since they were uncle-nephew and his present whereabouts were known by family. However, Bones was preparing for such an eventuality with a view to preventing it from interfering with his ambition.

Bones left the bookshelves, walked to the kitchen, poured a cup of coffee, carried it out to the narrow balcony, and sat down in one of the white plastic chairs. Ordinarily he was unaffected by such mundane things, but he admitted to himself that the view of the city, the coast, the harbor, the islands, and the seas beyond was one of staggering beauty. He knew too that it was the view that partly had led him to select this condo. It was partly the views that had attracted the earliest inhabitants, then the Greeks, Romans, and subsequent Neapolitans. The Romans had built enormous seaside villas nearby for the views and the convenience of proximity to the sea. Some of these had their own pools in which fish and shellfish were raised for food. A few still existed as ruins. Naples had had its ups and downs, its invasions and raids, its changes of governments, but had somehow survived all of them. The view, of course, always was intact.

Royalty occupied the palaces, money flowed in from commerce and taxes, and prosperity was the norm during the Kingdom of Two Naples years. Maria Christina, Marie Antoinette's sister, had been queen, a palace that rivaled Versailles had been built, Admiral Nelson was a hero to the populace, and Lord and Lady Hamilton - the famous Emma - were important personages. Foreign writers were seduced by Naples into writing effusively such phrases as "see Naples and die" and "Naples is a paradise." Young gentlemen from England finished their educations with a European tour, of which Naples was a major highlight.

And then, following the unification of Italy, the capital was moved to Rome, tax revenues were sent there too, and the city fell into depression. World War II was especially hard on the Neapolitans, with the fleeing Germans even burning the old city hall records. Advancing American soldiers found squalor and starvation in the bombed-out city.

But today, thought Bones, Naples is largely avoided by Americans who come to see the ruins of Pompeii on day tours from Rome or from cruise ships, and perhaps tour the Naples museum to see the artifacts, and then flee, having been filled with old stories of filth, poverty, and crime in the streets, all highly exaggerated. Naples still is beautiful, proud, and recovering from war and political neglect. Industry is active, the harbor is filled with ships, and the people look prosperous. It is the face of this recovered Naples that the politicians and inhabitants turn tentatively to the world today.

A knock at the door interrupted Bones' musings and he rose to go answer it.

* * *

The airport terminal in Naples is surprisingly small for a famous city of more than a million people. It has no "Welcome to Naples" atmosphere, just a scruffy functionalism. There is no inkling of the celebrated views, and it is located in one of the most crime-ridden sections of the city. Arrival at the airport, whether by air or land, is so unpropitious that it may arouse anxiety in new visitors who have been bombarded with stories of ripoffs and muggings in the city.

William Weston took a deep breath as his taxi left the terminal for his hotel, assuring himself that part of his dark mood was due to fatigue from the long flight and not just from exposure to the dreary airport. Still, he could not help comparing the neighborhoods they drove through after leaving the airport entrance with the slums that he had seen in Mexico. He closed his eyes for a moment as the taxi merged from the airport streets into a freeway. He unexpectedly dropped off to sleep. When he awoke a few minutes later, they were speeding along a seaside road. He sat up, looked around, recognized what could only have been Capri on the horizon, and then smiled, reassured. Yes, this would be a good trip. He had not been mistaken to come. Nepenthe. He was here. Let the adventure begin.

* * *

The Prime Numbers' flight had come in on time. They had settled into their hotel. Some had been for a walk on the nearby seaside street, others had taken naps, and now all thirty of them were having a drink in the little hotel bar before going out to a first dinner in Naples. Harry and George were at a table for two.

"Yes, nice to meet you too. I did see you on both flights, you know, but you were in first class and I was in tourist."

"Listen, Harry," said George, "you should have come with us for that walk. First down a little street right out of a movie set, then across a pretty park and the highway to a seaside sidewalk. What views—Vesuvius, Capri, the ships, the people, the air. I never expected that it really would be so glorious."

"Well, that's why we're here, I think. For the glory. When did you join the Prime Numbers, George?"

"Ah, yes, that. I moved to Palm Springs from San Francisco about a year ago. Retired bank manager. I heard there was a local gay men's social group called Prime Numbers of the Desert for older gay men 'and those who admire them.' I knew nobody, so I tried it and liked it. Mark's idea of a group of us seeing the Naples he knows seemed great, so here I am." Harry tilted his glass and drained the last of the wine. "Nice drink."

"Actually, George, the Prime Numbers is a national group of older gay men, with chapters in several states and tens of thousands of members. It is a godsend for people like us who retire and need a sense of purpose, especially if the retirement involves a move to a strange place. But wait, here we go, I think. It looks like Mark is about to say something."

* * *

Ethel Burns, an American of early middle age, was on a tour again, this time a moderately expensive Mediterranean cruise. As the huge ship passed between the breakwaters that form the long entrance into the Naples harbor, she stood with a group on the windy upper deck admiring the view of the approaching city. Jane, a fellow tour member next to her, who had been telling Ethel about her grandchildren, smiled and changed the subject.

"And now, Ethel my dear, enough of my boring grandmother stories. Tell me something about yourself. Is your husband with you?"

"Oh, no." Ethel replied. "I'm a widow."

Ethel always said she was a widow when she was on a tour. Her mother back in Des Moines had advised that as being the simplest solution to the embarrassing truth that her husband had left her for a man and moved with him to San Francisco. In Des Moines, of course, everyone knew the story, although they rarely mentioned it now to her, and over time her mother's friends largely had stopped patting her hand in sympathy whenever they met her with the usual kiss on the cheek. Still, it was a subject gossips would not let die, especially since her husband, John, had been a popular minister of their suburban church.

"Oh, I'm sorry. I hope you're not offended," said her neighbor.

"No, no. It's been some time now. I'm mostly resigned to it. Still, I do like to get away sometimes, like this trip. Very pleasant, isn't it? The sea, the air, the nice cabins, the service."

A double blast from the ship's horn startled them both. It was followed by a public address announcement about the ship's imminent docking in Naples and then a recording of a tenor singing "Funiculi, Funicula" in a reedy voice. Ethel and Jane said good-byes, parted, and joined the streams of other passengers returning to their cabins to change for a day ashore.

* * *

John Campbell had called friends in Naples soon after he had signed a contract to write the score and libretto for a Broadway musical about Woodstock. The friends had a cliffside estate in the west end of Naples in Posillipo, an upscale neighborhood on a hill above the bay. They had rented their very private guesthouse below the main house, with a good grand piano, to John, his wife Mary, and their daughter Helen for three months so that John could work on the musical without interruptions. Mary put eleven-year-old Helen in a local school to learn Italian and make friends with neighborhood girls.

This afternoon, John was at the piano, composing. He would play a few bars, stop to write it down, a few more bars, writing again, on and on. Outside on the garden lawn, his daughter and a dozen new Italian girlfriends from the school ran around and seemed to scream loudly at everything.

"Mary," John called to his wife in the kitchen. "Mary, please ask the girls to be a little quieter. I can't work very well with all this noise."

Mary went to the door and said, "Helen, don't scream."

Helen screamed.

"Please, Helen, don't scream."

The girls all screamed and laughed.

Helen formed them into a line and said, "Scream, scream, scream."

The girls screamed, screamed, screamed.

John joined Mary in the doorway and said, "Now, look here."

The girls screamed and laughed. "Dance," shouted Helen. "Dance and scream."

Helen joined the line and they all danced and screamed, "I scream, you scream, we all scream."

Then, with one last scream, they dropped into frozen curtsies that would make a ballerina proud.

Helen announced, "I'm teaching them to scream in English." And they all ran giggling down the garden steps and disappeared.

"I'm so sorry, dear. I will get this under control," said Mary sheepishly.

"Listen, Mary," John replied with his hand on his chin, "I might use that. Can you get them to do it again?"

* * *

After his arrival at the airport and taxi ride to the Hotel Vesuvio, William Weston had slept the remaining day and entire night through. He woke mid-afternoon in his luxurious suite, reportedly the one in which Caruso had died, and ordered a very late breakfast sent up. William liked older grand hotels, even though they sometimes were a little seedy. He had not looked forward to staying with his fellow Prime Numbers at the modestly priced little hotel that had been taken for them. When volunteers were requested to stay elsewhere because of overcrowding, he quickly had accepted, explaining that his hotel, the Vesuvio, was close by. It was a waterfront hotel in the Santa Lucia district, once a grand tour destination. Breakfast arrived with such good coffee that it wakened him thoroughly. He bathed, dressed, found his address book, and punched in a number on the bedside telephone.

"Marutus Taylor, please ... Oh, he's not ... Yes, William Weston ... He is? ... Five o'clock ... Yes, of course I can. I will be there at five ... Thank you. Good-bye."

Mutual friends had recommended that he look up Marutus Taylor whom they said was brilliant, handsome, and affable. Taylor was a Juilliard graduate with a brief performing career as a concert pianist prior to joining the San Carlo Opera as artistic director. So, in a few hours he was to meet the man himself for a drink at his home.

William had been unattached since his lover's death five years previously. The lover had been much older—indeed, William was still in his teens when they had been introduced on the gay beach in Santa Monica. The man was handsome, middle-aged, wealthy, had been everywhere and knew everyone, and was highly educated. He and William were attracted to one another almost instantly, and William had moved into his Santa Monica Canyon house within the week. The parents caused no trouble, recognizing the potential benefit to William. Over the next years, the two men traveled extensively, and William had enrolled in design schools in Los Angeles and New York. He had an innate flair for putting together seemingly disparate things that immediately turned into beautiful objects. The lover had similar tastes and encouraged William.

Eventually, William was able to apply his talent to events, starting with simple dinner parties at home based on the numerous gay Hollywood ones that he and his lover attended frequently. Over time, his dinner parties grew into larger and much more complex affairs that his imagination fueled—say, dinner guests arriving on the Santa Monica beach by a helicopter landing in a circle of bonfires and then being driven in limos up the nearby canyon to the house—and on into anniversaries for gay friends and then to marriages, receptions, and birthdays for gay and straight friends-of-friends, and ultimately to varied national conventions. Along the way, he became a Certified Special Event Professional and belonged to the International Special Event Society, which gave him access to vast numbers of event supplies at wholesale prices and a pool of talented assistants. He bought a studio in the industrial area of Santa Monica south of Olympic, a ten-minute drive from the house, in which many of the decorations were put together and many supplies were stored.

It amused him to block out an event in his mind, transfer it to paper, get the approval of the people giving it, hire talented assistants to do the footwork, see that everything was delivered and installed properly, and then stand by to ensure that nothing went wrong. Aside from delayed deliveries and inclement weather, there had been surprisingly few failures. It was fun for him, gave him a sense of purpose and accomplishment, brought him considerable praise, and—for a time—he enjoyed collecting the advance and final fees and paying the suppliers and staff. Now, he had a personal assistant who handled most of the money but only after close consultations with William. His fees were surprisingly large, and he kept them that way because it gave him a sense of personal pride; although, by this time, he did not need the money. Indeed, his tax accountant often pointed out to him that he lost an unreasonable amount of the fees to taxes because of his wealth and high tax bracket. Nevertheless, he would not hear of setting up a corporation just for tax purposes.

By the time of his lover's death, William had become a highly regarded designer. He had inherited the entire estate, with the exception of an enormous collection of Isadora Duncan memorabilia, which the lover had amassed passionately over decades. This went to the UCLA library archives ostensibly as a gift, but secretly the estate required a substantial payment of several millions.

William now specialized in parties, mostly for the rich and famous, and was widely sought for his work. He had a house and studio in Palm Springs too but traveled extensively, for instance twice in one recent month to Tokyo to provide flower arrangements for separate events. Acquiring him almost guaranteed the success of a wedding and reception, and mothers of brides could be cutthroat in obtaining him, especially valuing his innovations. At one such evening reception in Las Vegas, he had received sensational press for one item alone: thousands of enormous angel trumpet flowers underwater in the central floodlit pool surrounding the projected intertwined initials of the couple.

For the Prime Numbers on this trip, he had volunteered to improvise a simpler party or two in Naples. They were his friends. Curiously, he could not remember exactly who first had approached him about this. Tomorrow he would see Mark, the trip leader, about logistics. He envisioned a simple social gathering or two at spectacularly picturesque places and perhaps something at the home of a local gay man. In the beginning, his imagination had jumped almost immediately to an outside catered dinner high up on the lip of the Vesuvius crater, but he quickly and wisely realized that he did not have enough time or local contacts for something of this complexity. However, the challenge appealed to him, and a few years later, he was able to mount just such a dinner party on a warm and windless summer night, with the lights of candelabra and a full moon illuminating the vast crater on one side of the long table and the glittering city and shining sea on the other.

Although he had had brief affairs after the lover's death, William had not considered any of them to be serious. He was in his late forties, however, and knew that another partner would fill a gap in his personal life. It was partly to get away from the routine in Palm Springs and rethink his life that he had come to Naples.

He left his room and took the elevator down to the lobby.

"Hello," he said there to the smiling concierge, who looked up from a small desk in the lobby. "Can you advise me how to get from the hotel to this address?" He showed her the address that he had for Marutus Taylor.

"Ah," she replied. "Very nice place. I will call a taxi for you and you will be there in five minutes, perhaps, ten minutes at the most."

"Could I walk?" asked William. "I was on planes all day yesterday and walking a stretch would be wonderful now."

"Umm. Yes, I think so. It is about one and a half miles but very simple. You cross the street in front of the hotel to the sidewalk by the sea, turn right, stay on that sidewalk, and it will take you right to your address. The route will be flat and beside the beach until near the end, where you will pass a marina and then start up a hill, go by some beach clubs, and then watch for your building on the left. You may have to ask someone because street numbers aren't always so obvious in Naples."

So William set out on foot, passing places that appeared in sequence exactly as he had been told. Finally, a little way up the described hill, he hesitated at an opening to a parking area that had arches in a wall at the far end through which he could see the sea. There indeed seemed to be no number, no name, but a fellow who had been washing a car spotted him and came over, drying his hands on a towel and struggling into a jacket.

"Yes, sir?"

"Oh, hello. I am looking for Marutus Taylor."

"Your name?"

"William Weston."

The doorman, as he turned out to be, removed a cell phone from its holder on his belt, held it in his right hand, dialed a number with his thumb and, after a few words, returned it to his belt. He motioned for William to follow him.

"Please," he said, and led the way across the parking lot to the double-arched entrance that opened to a narrow porch with a low balustrade and view of the sea and sky, two shades of blue separated by a horizontal line. On the left side of the room inside the arches was a small elevator, door already open. The doorman stood aside for William to enter, followed him in, pressed a button, and nodded silently to him as they moved downward very slowly. William realized that the building was built into the sea cliff and that they were descending into it from the roof.

It was thus that William entered the legendary and fabulous Palazzo Donn'Anna for the first time.

* * *

What to tell you about Carl Craven? He grew up in an east Florida tidewater town, a deadly, anti-intellectual place, with a populace dedicated to keeping it that way. He was wholly uninterested in the traditional sports that consumed his male peers and early escaped into books, from which he learned that there was another world "out there." Smart, he had been advanced two years in grade school and graduated high school at age fifteen as a fetching, quiet young man with even features, an excellent figure, and a bright smile. His father, desperate to avoid the small-town scandal he feared that a handsome and fey son might cause, enlisted Carl in the army the week of his graduation. They lied a year about his age since back then you had to be sixteen years old to enlist and even then needed parental permission. So, Carl left Florida and went eagerly out into the world, returning over the years only for brief visits to his parents. He had eclectic interests, and this enthusiasm for new experiences and ideas was one of his chief attractions.

After the army stint, mostly in Japan, Carl lived for five years in Manhattan, sampling all the famous excitements of a candy shop for gay young men. Next, learning that San Francisco had a free junior college, he moved there and went through those two years, then transferred to the state university at Berkeley, where he eventually took a doctorate in geology, the field that interested him most. He then became an assistant professor at another campus of the same university in Riverside, southern California, not far from Palm Springs.

Life seemed good to Carl, almost complete. He had a progressing career, the respect of his university colleagues, and interesting research projects that he regularly completed and published. Still, there was the nagging doubt in his mind that had been there since he was a child: did he belong? Was he doing the right things? And he even had a strong sense that more was intended of him somehow. It wasn't just the feeling of otherness that many gay men experience; it was something more than that. An unknown seemed to be calling. He had long handled it by shrugging it off as the "my parents brought home the wrong baby" feeling that many gay men had. But it didn't go away.

Carl relished friendships with older gay men, perhaps a compensatory reaction to the early rejection by his father. On vacation visits to nearby Palm Springs, he had fallen in with some members of the Prime Numbers, who eventually had invited him on their Italian journey. The famous volcanic features of the Naples area intrigued him so that he had accepted and agreed to talk to the group about the volcanoes as needed. In preparation for the trip, he read quite a few technical papers and monographs about it with titles such as *The Eruptive History of Vesuvius, The Subsurface*

Geologic Structure of the Campanian Plain, The Morphology and Distribution of Italian Calderas, and the like.

So, now Carl was in Naples as part of this group, which hoped he might be able to explain puzzling geological features to them in a way that would be easy for them to understand.

11. LET THE GAMES BEGIN

It was a very stormy morning, with intermittent rain squalls, wind, thunder, and lightning. The sleek, silver bus merged to the right through noisy morning traffic, slowed for the exit sign that read "Lago d'Averno," entered the off-ramp, looped under the Naples to Rome freeway, and pulled into the wet parking lot of an overlook. With a hiss and a clank, the bus door jerked open, and a series of mostly portly older men descended to the pavement and gathered in a group at a low wall, below which a steep hill descended to a nearly circular lake. Mist drifted slowly over the lake, and a sulfurous smell rose in the morning wind and was remarked on by the men. It was the Prime Numbers at the very first group stop on their Italian journey.

"Sometimes you can smell a volcano before you can see it," commented one of the men.

"Quite right," replied Mark in a louder voice directed at the whole group. "That lake below is circular because it occupies the crater of a small volcano. The odor is gas rising from it. The lake is named Averno. The Greeks and Romans considered it to be the entrance to the underworld. Spirits of the recently dead gathered in silent, sad groups on the shores below us and waited for a boat poled by Charon to appear through the mists to take them to their final resting place deep underground, where they would remain forever in a peaceful and bodiless existence.

"Okay, now Prime Numbers, chip in with questions and thoughts so that we can keep this conversational and not turn it into just another boring tour guide lecture. Yes, George?"

"I don't think that any of us find your presentation boring, Mark," replied George. "Fill us in about what we are seeing and let us stop you if it is too much. What say?"

The other men nodded, and one of them said, "Hey, Mark, tell us what we're looking at. If you don't, then we won't know about it."

Mark smiled, looked down for a moment, then looked up again and spoke.

"Over the past twenty-five hundred years, quite a few bright men have stood where we are standing at this moment and in other places where we will be in the next few days. They wondered at the unusual things they saw, took memories away with them, and some of them worked these memories into the ancient myths and stories of great beauty that were told and retold by professional storytellers at homes, palaces, festivals, and in the streets of villages and cities. Some of these eventually were written down and have become part of classical literature.

"In a sense, we are ahead of them. We don't need their magical explanations involving gods and heroes. We have followed their great philosophical leads and investigated the real world so that we no longer make up superstitious stories to account for natural places such as this. On our trip, we have Carl Craven with us. As you know, Carl is a geology professor. There are many ways to appreciate Naples, but I do think that some knowledge of its geology is basic. Carl was available, and I jumped at the opportunity to have him with us. Naples without an understanding of the landforms, of the kinds of rocks present, of the volcanoes and their histories, and even of the underlying continental drift forces at work, would be a Naples inadequately understood. Carl, could you give us a first thumbnail sketch of the geology of the area? I think that the weather might not permit more."

"You bet," said Carl, stepping forward. "Unraveling the geology of the world is one of the great accomplishments of mankind. This whole area of Italy around Naples is called Campania. It is a great plain formed by sediments that lie above foundered blocks of the earth's crust. These blocks were cracked, formed, and sank at varying rates when Italy first was bent by continental drift forces long ago. Molten rock from below came up through the cracks around the great blocks and formed volcanoes, including the little one we are looking at below us. That is pretty simple, but this lake fills the crater of one of those volcanoes, a very small one that formed late in the long geologic history of this area. Nothing mysterious about the process at all. Perfectly straightforward. Is that enough for an introduction, Mark?"

"Great, Carl, perfect. You will have time in the days to come to fill in more. Some of the more curious old Greeks and Romans would have been delighted to learn what you have just told us. And yet, even today, there may seem to be something magical to us still in such a theatrical, steaming, vaporous, curious place so that one can see how its origin might have been attributed to a god such as Vulcan, who might have objected to being displaced so easily."

At that moment, there was a loud crack, a flash of lightning, and then a long, low rumble of thunder followed by a sudden pelting rain.

"See what I mean?" Mark shouted as the men hurried noisily through the sheets of falling water for the bus door and their seats.

* * *

Bones crossed the living room, putting his coffee mug down on the kitchen counter as he went, and answered the knock on the front door by opening it. A fat man, standing alone there, nodded to Bones.

"Enter, please, sir. Welcome," said Bones, stepping aside to give the man space and then closing the door.

The fat man walked to a sturdy couch and sat down heavily.

"I will be glad when your elevator is installed," he breathlessly said.

"Soon, I understand," replied Bones, sitting in a chair opposite him. "Coffee?"

"No, thank you. I came to assure you that I am only an observer. Let there be no misunderstanding."

"There is no misunderstanding," replied Bones.

The fat man nodded. "The time is soon. Are things ready?"

"Everything is in order," Bones responded. "The crypt below is being finished as we speak. And I am aware that he is near. You may rest assured that everything will be done as instructed."

"I never doubted that, but I needed this additional assurance." He heaved himself to his feet again and said, "Good-bye," with a salute.

"Good-bye, sir," replied Bones, also standing. "I am not to see you again."

"Ah, but that is an error. How is it possible for a Grand Master to err? We will meet once more."

"So?" replied Bones. "It will be."

They bowed to one another, almost imperceptibly. Bones moved across the room and opened the door. The fat man left, and Bones closed the door behind him. A slip of paper lay on the couch where he had been sitting.

* * *

Ethel had signed up for her cruise ship's tour to Pompeii, and now the participants were filing through the shade of the arched entrance to the Roman theater there. Someone tapped Ethel on the shoulder.

"Hello, Ethel. It's Jane. Remember we were talking on the upper deck early this morning?"

"Oh, yes, Jane. Of course I remember. How are you?"

"Well, we're a little warm and tired from all the walking. Ethel, this is my brother Hank."

Hank was fetching-looking in a country boy way. He was tall, very thin, with snake hips, long arms, big hands, an almost handsome face (his jaw wasn't broad enough for classically handsome), a twisted grin, and a lanky, plow boy walk. He was well preserved for his age, early fifties. Women still looked at him on the street—and elsewhere too. He and his sister were so little alike physically that the relationship seemed implausible to some people. Above all, Hank appeared to be nice, and that was a quality that Ethel understood. She liked him immediately.

"Good morning," said Hank, and reached out a hand, which Ethel took for a moment.

"We like Pompeii," he continued. "What about you, Ethel?"

"Oh, well," she answered. "I guess I like it too. It sort of reminds me of being in Japan on a tour last year."

"Japan? Pompeii?" asked Jane. "How's that, Ethel?"

They passed into the sunlight of the open theater and were forming into a tight group around the tour guide, a short woman waving a big tassel of red yarn tied to the end of a very tall staff so that everyone would know where she was.

"I thought that Japan was like Disneyland. You know, not quite real. Like something put together to amuse children."

Jane put a hand on Ethel's forearm. "Hank was just saying something similar about Pompeii. What was it, Hank?"

Hank took off his glasses and hat, wiped his brow with a handkerchief, and then put them back on.

"I don't think that Pompeii is like Disneyland. I just think that it is terribly dirty and run down. They should fix it up like they did Williamsburg. Now there's a place that gives you a real feeling about life in the past. People in period costumes walking around, pretending to go about their lives, and even answering questions from visitors as if they really were in the past. Now if they did something like that with Pompeii, then it would be a real success, don't you think? A few guys in togas or whatever they were called. Not this dirty, rundown affair that just looks like it needs a bunch of money to fix it up."

"Maybe," said Ethel. "Maybe, Hank, you should talk to somebody about that. I bet nobody ever thought of it."

"Attention, friends," called the tour guide. "I am now going to recite a few lines from a play called *Trojan Women* that once was performed right here, and then I want someone to tell me who wrote it. Here's a hint. He was a famous Greek playwright."

"Hey," Hank replied loudly to her. "They promised on the ship. No quizzes."

* * *

"Good afternoon."

It was a free afternoon for the Prime Numbers. Many had gone to Pompeii, since Mark had not included it in the places where he personally would take them. Carl had decided instead to look around Naples by himself and had left their hotel on Piazza Amedeo and followed streets toward what he knew from his tourist map was the royal palace area, memorizing street names so that he would recognize them on return and not get lost. Colonna, Mille, Filiangeri, and then Chiaia, a pedestrian-only street several blocks long bordered by shops. At the end of Chiaia, he had come upon a café with outside tables and paused, thinking he might have coffee. As he entered the outside privet-bordered enclosure looking for a free table, he passed a fat man, sitting alone, and holding a flute of wine.

"Good afternoon. Won't you join me?"

Instead of coffee, he had, at the fat man's suggestion, a glass of the same wine. The waiter also brought them a small dish of ice cubes, which were topped with what Carl thought must be olives with stems attached.

"Try one," said the fat man. "It is an acquired taste, but you may like it."

The texture and taste were decidedly un-olive, a crunchy texture and a salty, curiously musky taste that lingered on the tongue.

"Odd, but interesting. What are they?"

"Capers," the fat man replied. "You should learn to like them if you wish to understand Naples."

"I thought that capers were small things used in cooking."

"Ah, that is true, they are. But those are the buds of caper plant flowers, picked before blooming. These are the fruits of the same plant, usually called caper berries in English. Not widely eaten in America. More's the pity."

They talked pleasantly for an hour, first about the wine, which the fat man said was from an area north of Venice and made from a variety of grapes named prosecco. This particular wine was made from grapes that grew in a small hilly area there called Cartizze, where they had been highly prized since at least the sixteenth century, and was now produced by a young brother and sister team, both of whom he knew. They talked too about the history of their café, Gambrinus. And finally the fat man told amusing stories about his own past as a teenaged hustler in Hawaii in the Doris Duke days. Carl related something of his own life. It was all very pleasant, the more so because unexpected, with quite a lot of laughter. He found the fat man delightful.

"Perhaps you might like to walk across the street with me and let me show you the royal gardens?" the fat man then suggested.

And so, they did that, over to gardens behind a grand palace and an adjacent opera house, both of which Carl would become more familiar with later. The gardens were composed mostly of very mature exotic trees, really more of an arboretum than a garden, but there were gravel paths running between them and a few flower beds and flowing fountains. Everything was carefully kept up. It seemed very beautiful to Carl. The fat man explained the history of the gardens as they walked.

At last, the fat man said, "Carl, I have to leave you here. Perhaps we may meet again." They then shook hands.

"My pleasure," said Carl. "Thank you, sir. I hope that we will."

The fat man strode away and entered a rear door of the opera house, unseen by Carl, who left the gardens, easily found Via Chiaia, and retraced his steps to the hotel.

As he went up in the tiny elevator to his room, he thought again of the fat man.

"What a charming person. I should have asked how to reach him. I didn't even ask his name." And then he thought, "How did he know mine?"

* * *

The bed moved, and William woke but did not shift his position or open his eyes. He could hear Marutus moving quietly about, then open the door to the bathroom, turn on the shower, turn it off, return to the bedroom, and finish dressing when the shoehorn clicked against the heels of his shoes.

William felt exceedingly well and suspected that he was experiencing the initial release of biochemicals that create the love phenomenon in humans. His friend, the university biochemist, claimed to have isolated them but refused to publish the results because of potential damage to society. "Imagine," he had said, "gang drug dealers with this chemical on hand. The initiator that will cause the whole set of amphetamine-like effects called love. Imagine this chemical on call to anyone."

Certainly William felt excited and immensely pleased. He knew that if he did not encourage it, the chemicals would be neutralized and the feeling would disappear in days, weeks, or months. What to do? Marutus was very interesting and attractive. He was said to be trustworthy. He might make a near-perfect lover. William was aware that his emotions wanted him to go for it, but there was a strong intellectual side to him that urged caution. Would Marutus be a satisfactory long-term companion? Perhaps the thing to do was to proceed with cautious hope. After all, they had just met that day.

"William, *caro*, you awake?"

"Umm," replied William, looking up from the bed at a fully dressed Marutus and reaching out for his hand. "One more moment. It must be jet lag."

He hadn't meant to let this happen, but Marutus had seemed so familiar, like someone he had known for years, that it just had felt natural to hold onto his hand a second too long when Marutus came through the apartment door at last, shook hands with him, and kissed him quickly on each cheek Italian style. And then, being shown around the incredibly beautiful apartment and bumping shoulders with him from time to time as they moved about together was deliciously intimate, almost fraternal.

"So beautiful. This apartment is just so beautiful. I didn't expect anything like this."

"Oh," Marutus had responded, "it really is my aunt's doing. She was an aunt by marriage. If the Bourbon dynasty had lasted, she would have been a princess. Marie Antoinette was a distant cousin. My aunt had the place decorated by California decorator William Haines. I only added a few bibelots such as the Buddha. I always liked the comfort of the living room, really intimate, but not grand. It is a great place for conversation with a few friends. But parties go well here too. However, it really is the seventeenth-century building itself that is the highlight. The grandeur, the ruinous fairy tale quality, especially when viewed from the sea, and its association with the sea itself. Much of the foundation is underwater, you know. Very Naples."

Patrick, the valet, had shown William into the living room when he first had arrived, explaining that Marutus was at the gym and had called to say that he would be a few minutes late. Patrick had offered him a drink, which he had declined, but then after seeing the apartment with Marutus, they had settled down in the living room, he on a couch with tapestry-covered pillows behind him and Marutus in a chair in front of the Buddha statue, which backed his head like an ornate aura. Patrick had brought a tray with Campari and soda and disappeared. Marutus deftly had fixed each of them a drink.

"To an adventurous Neapolitan holiday for you," he had proposed as a toast. They had touched glasses and taken first sips.

Marutus' parents both had been killed in an automobile accident when he was quite young. His aunt had adopted him and saw him through the best schools in Naples, insisting that he have special attention in music and art. Later, he attended Cambridge University but withdrew eventually to enroll in the Juilliard School of Music. There he became a brilliant pianist but decided not to perform because of stage fright. His music teacher had been sympathetic and understanding. She told him, "Nothing matters ultimately but Bach and the garden." Wanting to stay in the music field, he returned to Italy and found an administrative place at Teatro alla Scala in Milan where he eagerly learned about running an opera house and eventually was advanced to a highly responsible position. From there, a move to the San Carlo Opera in Naples was natural, especially since his aunt had become a major donor there some years earlier with just this possibility in mind. When the aunt died, she left her entire estate to William. He continued at the San Carlo with great success. He traveled, met other men in the opera worlds, and had occasional affairs but had never taken a lover. Like William, he had been considering this possibility of late, thinking it was time to settle down a little more.

And now Marutus and William had been to bed. William turned his head and looked from the bed through the balcony open doorway out to the sea, darkening in the twilight, with lights coming on in the city, on the boats in the harbor, and on the islands.

"Babe, I have to be at the theater shortly. Would you like to stay here until I return? It will be very late. Or go with me? Or let me drop you off at the Vesuvio? It is on the way."

William stretched and smiled broadly. "I'd like to stay right here forever, but you can drop me off at the hotel. I'll be dressed in a minute."

"Alright," replied Marutus, smiling too. "But I want to see you tomorrow. I have something to show you. May I pick you up at noon?"

And so they reluctantly left the bedroom. William paused a moment at the doorway and looked back, thinking it would never happen again quite like this.

* * *

Blu Angels baths at 03:30, close by the Naples railway station. Inside, two thin, very black, Senegalese young men, dressed only with towels around their waists, stopped by the wall of a courtyard on the ground floor to help a third one climb over from the outside alley, stash his clothes, and pick up a towel from a bench before they all padded off barefoot and giggling toward a doorway, which they entered through dense clouds of steam.

"Uh-oh," said Harry to George. "Fire in the hold."

With mutual grins first, and then questioning eyebrow elevations, followed by affirmative nods to one another, Harry and George, who were out together for a night on the town and had been watching the illegal entry from a little distance, followed them in. In the morning, they would thank Mark for referring them to the establishment and tell him about their adventures in the steam room with excitement.

In the darkest shadow of the Blu Angel courtyard, a motionless fat man watched Harry and George enter the steam room. He smiled silently to himself.

111. THE LAST DAYS OF POMPEII

The Prime Numbers' bus left their hotel just before noon on a cloudless day, much later than usual, and merged into city traffic at the nearby Piazza Amedeo. They were served lunch on the bus as it sped across Naples to slower roads through the Pozzuoli and Baia areas, on to the base of Cape Misenum, then up a winding road on the hill that formed the cape, past modern villas and Roman ruins, into a tunnel, and finally out to a parking lot in the saddle between the point's uneven twin summits. Here the public road ended. Two vans awaited them in preparation for a planned event. These, and now the bus, were the only vehicles in the lot. Mark got out of the bus first and spoke to people by the vans who had been waiting for him. Together they walked over to the locked gate blocking a road leading to a lighthouse on the lower summit and talked for a few moments to uniformed guards posted there, explaining who they were and what they would be doing in case there was some objection. Mark then returned with his men to the bus and addressed the Prime Numbers, who were gathered around the bus doorway for the shade.

"Today is a special treat. I ask you to make the effort of hiking an unpaved trail to the very top of this point for it. The trail is a little rough because it is in a nature preserve, but it is not long and we are so near sea level that there is plenty of oxygen and today, happily, a cool sea breeze. Indeed, this point is nearly surrounded by the sea, as you have seen, almost an island. We will have to walk in single file most of the way because the trail is so narrow. Please go slowly, one step at a time. There is no rush. Enjoy the air and views on the way. There are some wildflowers too. We have jugs of iced water and fruit juice and chairs waiting for you in a clear area at the top of the hill. These young fellows will come with us and be at your service. If you wish, they will carry the light backpacks that some of you have. They will help you physically to the summit if you ask. Two of them will be the 'caboose' of our train and if there is a problem and you drop out, they will stay with you and, if need be, send for me at the head of our file and I will come back to help you myself. If you decide to return to the bus rather than proceed, that is okay. There is only the one trail, and the driver will be with the bus to let you inside.

"And, oh yes, these helpers are volunteers from ARCIGAY, Naples, our gay Neapolitan brothers. They wear name tags and all speak at least some English. They also are helping with logistics for a party for us later in the week, to be planned by our fellow member, designer William Weston, who is not with us now because he is off on the job. And we have promised them a party in Palm Springs whenever they visit California. And—attention, please—they have had considerable success nationally liberalizing laws against gay Italians. They wish to exchange information with us about this process. I know some of us are interested. Please speak to them about our gay freedom movement.

"And now men, *andiamo*, let's go. This way, please." And he led them onto the trail that passed up through the chaparral of the treeless hill, a long, colorful line of men in sunglasses, hats of various styles, and bright shirts blowing in the wind, all in great spirits, laughing and chattering to one another as they climbed up, quite easily it turned out, through the luminous sea air.

The time was early afternoon; the date was August 24.

* * *

A tall, good-looking young man carrying a soft black leather bag stepped down from the train from Rome after it arrived in Naples. He had a distinctly Gary Cooper aura, right down to long legs in Levis and boots, except for the head of hair, surely one of the brightest red redheads that Naples had seen in years. A black leather jacket was jammed between the two long handles of the bag. He walked with deliberation through the station to the street curb in front, raised one arm authoritatively, and got into the taxi that immediately pulled up before him.

"Grand Hotel Parker's," he said, and the taxi sped away.

* * *

Marutus introduced William to a young-looking man of thirty-something years in a huge room downstairs from the San Carlo Opera stage. All around them were portable racks with hundreds of costumes on hangers and boxes on shelves below containing wigs, hats, and other accessories. The place looked chaotic, but William knew that it could not be since these must be the costumes for the operas and ballets and a cataloguing system of some kind would therefore be necessary.

"Giuseppe is our new wardrobe master. When we finally decided to rearrange the costume collection and replace much of it, our longtime wardrobe mistress retired. Giuseppe too had just retired as one of our finest ballet soloists, and he was a godsend for the open position of wardrobe master."

William smiled at Giuseppe, shook hands with him, and looked at the tag on one of the hangers.

"I don't want even to begin to think how you keep any order here. It must be a madhouse during the season."

Marutus smiled, translated for Giuseppe, and replied, "No, not a madhouse, but very busy. We have never failed to dress a performer properly, although there have been some close calls. Part of our problem is space. All the costumes in this area, hundreds of them, have been replaced. We will soon be distributing these older ones to smaller performing groups throughout Italy. Meanwhile, I have an idea for the proposed party you told me that you want to arrange for your group. What about a costume party?"

William laughed loudly. "If you are going to suggest that we use some of these, it would be a fabulous success."

"Exactly what I am proposing. But Giuseppe and I don't want the costumes to go far for fear they might not be returned. Here is my plan. Outside the opera house is an enormous garden where we sometimes have receptions. Have your party there, and your friends could dress for it here, with the help of Giuseppe and a couple of his dressers, and then simply step outside for the party and return the costumes afterwards. We have tables, chairs, and lights that could be used for the party. Also a small stage. I will show you the garden in a few minutes."

William slapped his thigh and continued to smile. "You are an angel, Marutus. You too, Giuseppe." And he kissed them each on both cheeks. Giuseppe looked pleased.

"There's more," continued Marutus. "I would be honored to have you and your friends come to my apartment for drinks tomorrow night, after which we could go to dinner at a picturesque restaurant on the bay and sit outside right next to a marina. The weather should be beautiful. Very nice restaurant. I know the owner. He would arrange one long table for us, I think. The costume party could be later in the week."

"My god, cocktails at eight, dinner at nine, and a party later on. Who could ask for anything more? But now that you have done most of my work for me, what will I do with all the free time?"

"I have some ideas about that too," replied Marutus, with a sly look. "Let us go see the garden and then to lunch and I will tell you about them. Good-bye, Giuseppe. And thank you."

And Marutus and William left after shaking hands with Giuseppe.

* * *

"Is everyone comfortable?" Mark asked in a loud voice.

Around him in a loose semi-circle were the Prime Numbers and the ARCIGAY men, standing, sitting in aluminum chairs, even sitting on the ground. They had admired and photographed the panorama from the summit of Cape Misenum, a 360-degree mixed seascape and landscape of the Tyrrhenian Sea, the Naples area, and the many islands. All the places from Ischia to Vesuvius and Capri had been identified to their satisfaction. They knew where they were and what they were seeing. They were exhilarated by the setting. Everything was photographed repeatedly.

"Today," Mark continued, "we are going to deviate from the usual conversational approach of our tour and do something more formal: a reading. I want to tell you why. First, wealthy Roman gentlemen often were read to by Greek slaves when they were outside in places such as this. I want you to understand what that luxury might have been like. Second, one of them wrote two letters about what happened to him somewhere on this very point of land almost two thousand years ago. Third, one of our members, Greg here, as you well know, is noted in the theater for his excellent voice. He has copies of those old letters that he will explain and read to you. Greg."

Greg replaced Mark before the group and cleared his throat.

"Pliny the Elder essentially was secretary of the Roman navy, which was quartered in that harbor right down there. He had a villa somewhere below us on this cape, probably near the road on which we drove up. Pliny was a highly respected Roman patrician, a scholar, and a public servant, at the service of the emperor and the Roman government. He also was very wealthy. His nephew, called Pliny the Younger, lived with him and wrote the two letters I am going to read to you. The nephew had been asked by a Roman historian named Tacitus for these letters in order to complete a biography of the uncle. They were written a few years after the events described, but their veracity is impeccable. They are the only eyewitness accounts of the eruption of Vesuvius that buried Pompeii. I think that the letters mostly are self-explanatory. After I read them, we will take questions, 'we' including our geologist Carl over there, who will answer anything you may want to ask about the Vesuvius eruptions. Carl, stand up. Thank you. The two days the letters report on are August 24 and 25, 79 A.D. Today also is August 24, so the same day in 79 A.D. may have begun very much as our own day did, up until about this time.

"And now let me read:

"To Cornelius Tacitus. Thank you for asking me to send you a description of my uncle's death ..."

The audience then listened almost raptly to the long recitation, which ended with the sentence, "Of course, these details are not important enough for history, and you will read them without any idea of recording them; if they seem scarcely worth putting in a letter, you have only yourself to blame for asking for them."

Greg then closed the paperback volume of Pliny letters amid applause from his audience. Mark joined him.

"Thank you, Greg. No, stay here, please. And Carl, you come over with us. Now, the questions. Have at us, men."

A hand shot up, and a balding man named Leo spoke.

"Now, as I understand it, this eruption came out of that volcano, Vesuvius, way over there on the other side of the bay. Do you mean to tell us that this young guy Pliny and his mother were on this very hill and the ashes fell on them here, from the volcano way over there, so deeply that it buried everything like snowdrifts? That what he said? Isn't that a stretch? How far away is Vesuvius? Looks a long, long way to me."

"Carl," said Mark. "You take this?"

"Yes," replied Carl. "Pliny is correct. The ashfall from the 79 A.D. Vesuvius eruption has been identified in this area. It may look farther to you from here to there because of the landscape, I don't know. Actually, Vesuvius is only about twenty miles away in a straight line. It blew the ashes straight up, and the winds carried them over here. If you are still skeptical when we get back to Palm Springs, then let me take you all on a hike to the nearby Indio Hills and show you a thick ash deposit there that came from the eruption that formed Long Valley, next to the Mammoth Mountain ski area, about three hundred miles north of Palm Springs. That ashfall traveled much farther."

"When did this Long Valley eruption take place?" someone else asked.

"Seven hundred sixty thousand years ago. An absolute date, based on radioactive decay of elements in the ash. That ash fell all over the west, hundreds of miles from the source."

Another hand shot up.

"What's this about earthquakes and the sea coming in and out here during the Vesuvius eruption. What caused that?"

"Well," continued Carl with a nod from Mark, "the molten lava is moving around underground, pushing against the solid rocks, shaking them, lifting them up in places where it suddenly pools in big chambers below ground, letting the rock layers down again when the lava moves elsewhere or blows out of the volcano and the pressure is taken off. When the sea floor moves up in shallow water, the water flows away; when it moves down again, the water returns. Maybe sea water ran into the lava chamber too."

Someone else stood up.

"Listen, I got all that, you guys. But what was this business about both the uncle and nephew having baths and reading books while all this was going on? Why didn't they just run like hell?"

"That's mine," said Mark. "I want you to understand what civilized gentlemen these Romans were. They wanted to set an example to calm the hysteria of people around them. They felt the responsibility to do that."

Another hand went up.

"Gary?" asked Mark.

"Okay, so there is a lot of history here. I get that. What does the name mean, Misenum?"

"Remember that Aneas, one of the warriors who fought in the Trojan War according to myth, came here afterward by boat? He had a trumpeter named Misenus who supposedly drowned just off the beach below us somewhere, and the place has had his name ever since."

"That must have been very tragic, losing a shipmate like that."

"Yes, for him it was an odyssey gone wrong."

"You know, all of us Prime Numbers here are engaged in modern odysseys with you as our captain. Let nothing go wrong with that."

"It wasn't the *Odyssey*. I shouldn't have used that word in the journey sense. It was the *Aeneid*, but we know that you mean, I hope."

"When did Misenus drown?"

"Well, since the Trojan War was about 1250 B.C., it was sometime after that."

"More than three thousand years ago? That's some record. Can it be reliable?"

"Perhaps. The Roman poet Virgil, who lived in Naples toward the end of the first century B.C., includes this drowning in his long poem, the *Aeneid*, and apparently accepted it."

"I'm very impressed. Thank you."

"Who was the Roman emperor when Vesuvius blew up?" someone else asked.

"Let's see, 79 A. D. That would have been Vespasian, near the end of his reign, yes? No, Titus. Vespasian died in the summer. Anybody know for sure?"

"Why did they kill Julius Caesar?"

"I would like to stick to the subject here. Julius Caesar was assassinated more than a hundred and twenty years before the eruption of Vesuvius. At that time, the Romans apparently did not even know that Vesuvius was a volcano. But to answer your question, he was thought to be a threat to the Republic, about to declare himself king or emperor."

"Was that true?"

"Very likely. His heir, Octavian, eventually did exactly that. Some ancient writers even hint that they killed the wrong man or that they should have assassinated them both."

"But Octavian became the Emperor Augustus, a great man, wasn't he?"

"Yes, yes, he did many great things. But he also destroyed the Roman Republic."

"And caused Cleopatra to kill herself?"

"Very likely. Do not underestimate the influence of that very special lady on world history. She was the most famous woman and the most influential woman ever. Ever! But—please—let's get back to 79 A.D. That's why we're here today."

"I have a question, Mark."

"Yes, John. Give it up."

"So, this is the famous Baiae, the playground of the Romans?"

"Not up here, not on the cape, but on that strip of land we drove over to get here. The sand spit, below the tunnel."

"And the baths, famous for lusty men and women?"

"Long gone, only a few ruins remain. And some cheap modern restaurants."

"Everything passes, yes? Even such famous pleasures. Why?"

"Don't let's spoil our day with sad speculations and conjectures. Think of the famous Baiae as you have read about it. Exciting, infamous, debilitating, glorious. For gay men and women as well as straights."

"Like Las Vegas?"

"Probably better."

The questions continued for a time, then stopped and, at Mark's signal, everyone stood and the group filed back down the trail to the parking lot, some carrying chairs and coolers. Everyone agreed that Mark had created a great stop. The Prime Numbers and the Italians said good-byes, all the vehicles disappeared into the tunnel, and the vacant parking lot was reclaimed by the late afternoon winds that swept Cape Misenum.

* * *

"Is that wine good for you, Ethel?"

At his sister's suggestion, Hank had asked Ethel out to dinner in town since their cruise ship would be one more day in Naples. Ethel had accepted, and they had found a little restaurant near the port and settled in at exactly 6:00 PM, the time Ethel had said that everyone should have dinner.

Ethel wore a jersey skirt of a perfectly livid hue that almost exactly matched Hank's complexion. He had been seasick the whole cruise even though the sea was very calm, an old problem he later told Ethel, explaining that even the idea of a ship made him feel nauseous. Hank's brown trousers and beautifully wrinkled tan linen jacket, both selected by his sister, somewhat offset Ethel's gauche mauve blouse with mutton-chop sleeves.

"Oh, here," she said. "Let me just try it. Oh, my, too dry. Where is the sugar bowl?" she asked, looking around.

The waiter came when Hank motioned for him and they finally made him understand that they wanted sugar. He brought them a dish of it and Ethel emptied a heaping teaspoon of sugar into her wine, stirred it so vigorously that the spoon clanked loudly against the glass, and then tasted it again.

"Ah. Better, much better," she commented and then asked, looking around at the room in which they were very early customers, "How do they make any money with these empty restaurants?"

Hank shrugged, and they started the antipasto course.

* * *

John Campbell paused outside the simple doorway to the administrative wing of the San Carlo Opera, next to the grand entrance, to wave good-bye to his wife, who was being driven away by their landlord for an hour of shopping. Their car narrowly avoided two motor scooters that were riding side-by-side and then quickly was hidden from John's sight by a red city bus for tourists that had an open upper deck filled with sightseers from a cruise ship. John turned and entered the building, walked down a long hall, up a half flight of stairs, and stopped at a counter that had several clerks talking to customers before it. It took a moment for him to find assistance.

"Yes, may I help you?" The woman behind the counter asked him, "You are American?"

"Exactly," replied John. "Yes, I want to arrange to rent a studio."

"You do understand that this is an opera house?"

"I do, yes, but I was told that you rent studios too. I am writing a musical for production on Broadway, and I need something simple, like a dance studio—mirrors, a piano. And I would like to engage three singers from your school, if that is possible, to block out some scenes."

"Great," said the clerk. "Here is Mr. Solferino just passing. He is the person to whom you need to speak."

"Sir," she called to the man, who stopped beside John.

So John and Mr. Solferino looked quickly into a room where a men's professional ballet class was underway, sat down in a nearby office, and worked out the contract that John desired. One-hour sessions twice a week for a month in the same room. John was to bring a copy of his music for each of the singers, his wife would play, and he would test some scenes.

"What," asked Mr. Solferino, filling in the printed contract, "is the title of your musical?"

John smiled broadly and replied, "Scream."

"Okey dokey," said Mr. Solferino, handing John a copy of the contract. "We will see you Monday."

* * *

Ethel turned to Hank as they paused outside the restaurant.

"Oh, Hank. What a lovely dinner. Thank you so much. I don't know when I've had such fun."

Hank made a deep, mock bow toward her, stood erect again, pointed to his nose, and raised both eyebrows.

"What is it, Hank? Something wrong with your nose?"

He shook his head negatively, spread an open palm under his chin, and looked around as if seeking something.

"Charades?" asked Ethel. "We're playing charades?"

Hank nodded a vigorous yes and repeated his moves as they walked slowly toward the pier. A passing couple looked at him and laughed.

"Pulcinella," the woman said.

Then Ethel put a finger to her lips. "Smell? Yes, you smell something and wonder where it comes from? Ah, it's incense. I smell it too. That's it. Incense. I love incense."

"Correct. You win the game Ethel," replied Hank. "And I love incense too, but where is it?"

"Oh, look, Hank. There on the corner. That woman."

And, indeed, there on the corner was a woman seated on the sidewalk, a burning stick of incense in a lump of clay before her and boxes of it neatly stacked for sale. Hank and Ethel walked over to her.

"Two, please," Hank requested, holding up two fingers. He gave her a five euro note and she handed him the two boxes, one of which he immediately presented to Ethel and the other he placed in his jacket pocket.

"Shall we go back to our magic ship, milady?" he asked Ethel with a laugh. And so they did go back to the ship. Ethel was so pleased that she wanted to skip.

IV. COCKTAILS AT EIGHT

"Hank," asked Ethel when the dawn's early light from the porthole woke her, "do I snore?"

* * *

Mark had booked the Prime Numbers into their boutique hotel partly because it had almost the exact number of rooms for his group. In addition, the furnishings were somewhat elegant, the general ambience suitable for a gay group, and the Chiaia district hotel location was excellent. The hotel occupied the fourth and fifth floors of a six-story building a few steps from the convenient Piazza Amedeo. The double name—Hotel Booker-Marchesi—referred to a nineteenth-century couple who founded it, one English, one Italian, and Mark imagined that they had been gay men, but he never cared enough to inquire. The hotel was excellent for his purposes, and it served a breakfast that was perfect for everyone.

Today was another day and another breakfast in the hotel. The young waiter, Gianni, was busy serving coffee, tea, croissants, jam, cereal, yogurt, fruit, and rum babas, an early feast for the Americans. The sun was streaming through the windows, and the room was filled with good smells, laughter, and pleasant chatter at all the tables.

"I had no idea, just no idea. Pizza can be good, light, fresh, delicious. All I've ever had at home is the cheesy stuff that college boys gorge. Sticks to your teeth. What we had last night was a gourmet dish."

"Yes, and the crowds of people, all ages, packed in those alleys. What did Mark call it? The *passeggiata*? Everyone at the end of the day walking or just standing and talking. In crowds. We could hardly get through in places. Not drinking, not drugging, not watching anything electronic, just talking. Some came on motor scooters, and there was that one place where they suddenly all got on their scooters and just disappeared, the whole crowd."

"My dear, you missed that shop? Just before the restaurant? A hole-in-the-wall place with one kind of thing for sale: a shirt. One pattern, three sizes, nothing else. The material was gauze but in ten mad but soft-hued colors. Dyed after they were made; I checked the seams. I'm going back to get one of each. What an idea."

The desk clerk from Cairo looked in the doorway, caught Mark's eye, and mimed "telephone," little finger and thumb extended, middle three fingers in the palm, thumb at his ear, little finger at his mouth. Mark went to him, they disappeared into the reception area, and when he returned, he clapped his hands twice to get attention.

"Okay, men, here's the skinny. No bus. It's in the shop, and they hope to have it for us by late afternoon. So, change of plans. No Cuma or Cave of the Sibyl today. We will do that another day. Backup plan one is in effect. We will go on the metro from the station right here on our piazza two stops to the National Archaeological Museum, where I will show you two objects that define the sophistication and intellectual advancement of ancient Rome for me. We will also see all the Pompeii treasures. Then we'll go by open deck tourist bus to the Royal Palace down by the bay.

"Finish breakfast, meet me as usual in the lounge, same time. However—attention, please—today no camera bags, no clutches, no fanny packs. Cameras that fit in a pocket, wallets in front pockets, hands on them. We don't want to attract thieves on the metro. They are a real danger."

Mark then sat down again with Harry and George to finish his yogurt but almost immediately stood up again.

"Oh, yes. Our friend William has been busy. Tonight we will have cocktails in a private home and then dinner afterwards at a seaside restaurant. Casually dressy. Be ready to leave for that at 7:30. I will remind you again this afternoon."

* * *

The relationship between William and Marutus had begun with an early intensity. Simply put, these two men now found themselves unexpectedly, hopelessly, madly in love with one another and trying to be mature about it. They almost glowed when together. It was not an inconvenient time for either one of them. Each had successful careers, and being in love was an extra blessing.

William moved into Marutus' apartment, where they lived like newlyweds. Marutus left for work at the opera late afternoons or early evenings, and William sometimes went with him. More often he joined the Prime Numbers for dinner at some restaurant.

With the cocktail party for the Prime Numbers at Marutus' apartment imminent, William formed an idea for a floral design at the building entrance. So, with Marutus still in bed, he set out very early that morning with Patrick for the flower market that opened daily at dawn in the dry moat of the Castel Nuovo. Patrick spoke fair elementary English and, with William's rudimentary Italian, they were able to talk a little on the drive there in Marutus' car. William explained what he wanted to do for that night, and Patrick told about some of his experiences with previous cocktail parties in the apartment.

At the market, near the end of the second long row of stalls, they encountered an elderly vendor with buckets of spectacular Banksia flowers, beautifully colored and nicely fresh considering that they had been flown in from Holland. With Patrick's help, William went through the transaction of buying a great bunch of them, and they drove with them back to the apartment. Patrick took the flowers to the kitchen with instructions from William to trim the stems again and place them in water. William returned to a sleeping Marutus, who had not even missed him, stripped, got back in bed, and went to sleep again himself.

* * *

Mark led the Prime Numbers through the front doors of the National Archaeological Museum, surrendered a packet of tickets to an attendant who led the group through a pair of low, swinging wooden doors and then into the side entrance of a special exhibition titled "Eureka: Genius in Antiquity." They had entered an advanced part of the exhibit. Mark paused beside a glass exhibition display case and drew a semi-circle in the air before himself so that his followers gathered there.

"Now, I want you to look carefully at the objects inside this case. Don't look like much, huh? Just bunches of little metal wheels covered with greenish incrustations. Originally it was one mass, but that was broken in handling. This came from a probable Roman shipwreck found off the Greek island of Antikythera in 1900 by sponge divers and afterwards was brought to the surface by archaeologists. It has been firmly dated as first century B.C. The cargo of the ship suggests that it was looted from a temple or temples and was being taken to sell in Rome or maybe for use in a triumphal parade. There were wonderful art pieces such as bronze and marble statues, the marble ones nearly ruined by sea water, boring clams, and other marine animals very like the damage we saw the other day to the temple columns in the park at Pozzuoli. The bronze statues, however, were readily cleaned and have become some of the most familiar of ancient statues to us. The ship also carried wine, pots, jars, small bronze statues, jewelry, and utensils.

"The little mass before us simply was put aside as a curiosity.

"In 1974, a professor of the history of science at Yale published the results of his study of the Antikythera device, as it has become known, in a seventy-page scientific monograph put out by the American Philosophical Society in Philadelphia. Look carefully at the objects in the case. The little wheels are actually gears with cogs and Greek writing on them. They originally were encased in a wooden box that had collapsed, leaving the gears lying against one another in some disarray but not enough so that their original positions couldn't be reconstructed.

"The professor did this with x-rays and every means at his disposal. What he found was so astonishing that he himself wrote that the object might have been left by extraterrestrials.

"It is a computer. A computer with differential gears. Handmade with saws and files from a sheet of a simple kind of bronze. It was in use long enough so that several repairs had been made with lead solder. The computer, hand operated by turning a knob on one side, showed the positions of the sun and moon and, it was later found, other planets. It was made about 87 B.C., perhaps on Rhodes. This discovery changed the concept of the degree of sophistication of technology in ancient Greece and Rome. It is the oldest such complex device known.

"There were other things he wrote about it too, all in his monograph, a copy of which I have in my room and which I will hand out for you to pass around and examine when we get back. For the moment, I want you to get a look at the real thing and then to think about intellectual advancement in the evolution of human beings. At least by ancient Greek and Roman times, the human brain was advanced enough to be capable of conceiving and constructing computers. People of earlier civilizations perhaps were not. Certainly nothing in the vast numbers of objects retrieved from Egyptian tombs suggests that they were so advanced.

"And now we will go to the top floor and examine another metal object buried by Vesuvius in 79 A.D. that also is insight into another aspect of ancient civilization.

"On the way, we quickly will pass a great marble Roman statue known as the Farnese Atlas. It was found in the Baths of Caracalla in Rome. This Atlas holds a sphere that represents the dome of the sky with the then positions of the constellations shown. These, of course, change over time because the universe is expanding and stars move. The positions shown on the Atlas sphere correspond with those of the Antikythera device for the same time.

"Sorry about the lecture. Today is a little rushed because of the change of plans. We can talk about all of this at a later time.

"So, this way, please gentlemen, and don't lag around the Atlas statue, which I will point out to you. You will have time later to come back and admire his attributes, fetching if you like 'em big and muscular and hairy—in effect, bears."

* * *

"Listen, George," said Harry as they walked up the palatial interior stairs of the Archaeology Museum to the top floor with the group, "We're so far ahead today of those old Roman guys that I don't know why Mark even wanted to show us that primitive little machine."

"Oh, yeah," said Carl, who was just behind them. "Darling, when was the last time you lighted the pilot of your hot water heater?"

They all laughed.

* * *

"OH MY GOD."

The conversation volume went up dramatically, there was a lot of laughter, a couple of catcalls, and a scattering of applause as the Prime Numbers crowded around an exhibit on the upper floor of the Archaeological Museum.

"See, Butch, I told you art could be fun."

"Whoever owned this was one of us."

"Enough foreskin to hang themselves with."

"Must have been a zucchini planter."

The object of all this attention was, in fact, an elegant, ancient, large tripod charcoal brazier. The legs were formed by three satyrs, each sporting a prominent erection, one hand saucily on a hip, and the other hand thrust straight forward with the palm turned out, a clear warning to keep back.

"This," said Mark, "was a charcoal brazier. Free-standing. Tall enough to loaf around and warm your hands over. The material is bronze, the artist is unknown, but it is a masterpiece of sophisticated design, casting, and humor. It may be unique. The workmanship is impeccable. It was discovered in the buried Villa of the Papyri, not too far from Herculaneum, the same villa that Getty recreated in Malibu. This is probably the most sumptuous intact estate found to date in this area and is thought to have belonged to Julius Caesar's father-in-law, Lucius Calpurnius Piso Caesoninus. Since Caesar himself had a villa at Baia near our Cape Misenum, it is probable that he was at times a Piso guest and may have warmed his hands over this brazier. I imagine that his reaction on seeing it first time would have been similar to our own: delight.

"For me, this one object demonstrates that the Romans perhaps were intellectually as modern as we are and that we would have an immediate intellectual empathy with them if we could be transported back to that time. The Greeks had a continuous culture preceding the Romans, and this applies to them too.

"I have seen nothing comparable from much older civilizations, say the Egyptians. The Egyptians seem to me to have been without whimsy, living willingly in a society dominated by priests, building those huge, meaningless buildings, the ruins of which dot present-day Egypt.

"And now, your comments and observations. Workmanship, design, modeling, price. Give it up. Suppose this piece came up on *Antiques Road Show?*"

* * *

Visiting Professor Frank Bones surveyed his new office in the geology department at the University of Naples, a rabbit warren of buildings in many styles, a few of which were from the thirteenth century, the year the university was founded. He did a mental check: desk, two chairs, computer station, telephone, bookcases, work table. Adequate, if spare; just the way he liked it. Minimalism. In the hall outside the office door, four locked metal specimen cases contained plant material that had been found at Pompeii, Herculaneum, and other sites buried by the 79 A.D. Vesuvius eruption. In addition, he himself soon would collect sediment samples from the bottoms of ancient Roman garden ponds for pollen and perhaps entire leaves, flowers, fruit, and branches. He had access to the departmental geological laboratory and its staff for preparation. The university library would supply any references he did not already have in his personal research library.

Yes, he could complete the monograph promised in his application within the year. Then it would be up to the university to get peer reviews, return it to him for a rewrite, and then to publish it.

The departmental chairman had visited him, and he also had been to his first faculty staff meeting. They had assigned him a student assistant. A wall display case in the nearby Paleontology Museum had been reserved for him to exhibit some specimens for his work while in residence. He had been invited to teach a seminar in the second half of his tenure.

It was going well. If he could establish a strong enough academic and political presence in the department during this year, he might obtain a permanent professorship. He had sensed the anticipated opposition at the departmental meeting because he was not an Italian citizen, but none that seemed very effective. His ultimate goal was to publish a series of papers on the paleobotany of the entire Campanian area using specimens from its great thickness of marine and terrestrial sediments. The Vesuvius project was simple by comparison, a means to an end; a start. At home, he had the private number of the university president, left with him by his fat friend, with the notation that he should give the man a call and arrange a meeting to explain his desired program. He would do that soon.

Bones picked up his briefcase, which held some documents for foreign workers in Italy he needed to review that night, and, leaving the office, he turned out the light and locked the door behind him. On his way out of the building, he stopped and said a few words to the attractive middle-age departmental secretary, an important potential ally. As he walked away from her desk, she glanced admiringly at his broad shoulders and narrow hips and then stroked the roof of her mouth with the tip of her tongue before returning to her computer.

* * *

"Will you look at the dogs."

The Prime Numbers had ridden on the top deck of the red tourist bus from the National Archaeological Museum to the architecturally impressive Galleria Umberto I, walked through that, and then crossed the street to the side entrance of the Royal Palace. There, they had seen the grand staircase, the royal apartment, the chapel, the theater, and the the many kitsch bibelots seemingly beloved by royals everywhere, the monumental paintings on walls and ceilings, the tapestries, the views from the enormous deck at the harbor end of one floor, the various libraries (a glimpse), and now they had exited the main entrance into the Piazza del Plebiscito to view the palace facade for the first time.

"Yes, lordy, look at the dogs," exclaimed George. "Any city that loves its dogs like this is a place after my own heart. Mark, I withdraw all reservations about Naples."

And indeed there were dogs, dozens of them of every breed from great dane to cocker spaniel, gamboling together in playful groups or sitting and watching or sleeping, scattered all over one of the grandest piazzas in Europe. A recent bright mayor had turned the grand Piazza del Plebiscito into a pedestrian area where various events were held, even rock concerts. People brought their dogs to romp freely, and many stray dogs too ran free. Most people in Naples walked their dogs on leashes, but enough did not in this piazza to create the world's grandest dog park.

"Indeed, George, and all of you, Neapolitans love their dogs. Some of these no longer have owners but still they are fed by volunteers and also given rabies shots and are spayed. The animals are quite exceptionally friendly.

"But now I want you to turn around and pay attention to the facade of this building, the reason we came out here. There are a series of large niches in it, and each one has a statue of a former king of Naples. Come with me this way, it is the last one down there that I think will be of most interest to you."

So they all walked along with Mark to the far end of the facade and paused with him at the last niche.

"This statue is of Murat, one of Napoleon's greatest generals. As a reward, Napoleon made him King of Naples and married him to his sister. This king had style and wit, as you can see from his uniform, and also notable family jewels, as you can see too. Still, his wife ran around on him, much to the amusement of the people of Naples.

"Murat loved his uniforms. He was known to lead charges into battle while dressed in ostrich feathers and diamonds. Perhaps he would have gotten along with our own flamboyant General Patton. I have a print of a painting of Murat by Gerard that hangs in the Louvre. He is dressed in a flashy Hussar uniform, showing off a splendid great ass in his skin-tight trousers. I will bring it to breakfast in the morning.

"And now, friends, let us go around this end of the palace to the rear parking lot, where I am told that our newly repaired bus awaits us. We then will go back to the hotel and have about three hours before we meet in the lobby as usual at 7:30 to go for cocktails at the private apartment I told you about this morning. Afterward we will have dinner at a restaurant in a marina. Perhaps you might wish to spiff up your dress just a little."

And so they all followed Mark, except for a few laggards who paused for last photographs of the great general and his great basket.

* * *

"No."

John and Mary were discussing their daughter Helen during the morning coffee break that John daily took from his work. They were at a table on the patio, in the shade under an awning. Helen was at school.

"But John, she only asked for ballet lessons. That is an ordinary thing for girls of her age."

"She asked for ballet lessons because you told her that we would be working in an empty rented ballet studio some mornings. She now thinks that I have bought a ballet school. You let her believe this."

"But couldn't we take her with us? I'm sure that the school would let her out for this."

"Look, Mary, I deliberately reserved this studio during Mary's school hours so that you and I could go there and work quietly. I do not know when or where the opera's ballet classes are held and do not care. Mary would have to enter a beginners' class. These classes last longer than the hour for which we have the studio rented and surely are not at the same time. My work comes before our daughter's juvenile whims."

"She seemed so set on it. I hate to disappoint her."

"Our daughter is mindless, Mary. She suddenly becomes enthusiastic about something she hears about and forgets it very quickly. Tomorrow it will be something else. No."

"But what will I tell her?"

"Tell her that if she doesn't work harder at trying to help us with our lives that we will put her up for adoption."

"Oh, John. What a thing to say."

"But the idea has its attractions, you know. She is a selfish, thoughtless, manipulative girl and one day will be a selfish, thoughtless, manipulative woman who may place us in an institution at first opportunity in our old ages so that she can grab our money."

"Absolutely untrue, John. She is perfectly normal. This is just a stage. Perhaps she just could watch a ballet class and then explain to her friends at school about dance."

"Perhaps she is perfectly normal, but you could think about working on her some for my sake or I just might mention adoption to her myself. Life, Mary, is for adults. Children will have their chances later. And as for her addressing her class on the subject of dance after a visit to view a few ballet lessons, I think you know how I feel about unqualified people doing that kind of thing in schools. It's ludicrous. Remember the teacher at Helen's school at home letting her gay friend talk to Helen's class about roses because he—wasn't the word he used liked?—liked roses. Liked. Didn't know a damned thing about botany or horticulture. Wasn't qualified to do that by state law, a good law, and the teacher didn't go through the process to get the principal's approval because she knew he wouldn't approve. Rightly so. And we had to go to all that trouble to see that he couldn't do it again because there were other things he—ah—liked. In this case, Helen knows nothing about dance and never will. Let it go, Mary; let it go."

* * *

As the bus turned off the street to the Palazzo Donn'Anna, its headlights raked the arches of the top floor at the far end of the dark parking lot. Mark got out first and pointed the way to the entrance for the other Prime Numbers. There, in the center of the open foyer, William had placed a small marble table on which a great silver bowl held a tall arrangement of the Banksia flowers, illuminated by a single ceiling spot and backed by the black bay with glittering strings and groups of lights of the cities on the far shore and islands.

"Will you look at that. Weston is such a drama queen."

"You don't like the flowers? I was just thinking how beautiful they are."

"No, no, of course they are beautiful. Everything he touches becomes beautiful. I just meant who else would have the imagination to incorporate the evening lights of Capri into a flower arrangement?"

The Prime Numbers, carefully dressed for the occasion, milled about the foyer and adjacent balcony over the sea as they waited for the uniformed doorman to take them down in the small elevator, a few at a time, to the apartment where Marutus and William welcomed each group as it came through the door. William made the introductions and Marutus directed them to the living room where Patrick and an assistant manned a bar and another young man passed a tray of food. When the last of the guests had entered, William gave a thumbs up to the doorman, who disappeared as the elevator door closed. He then shut the front door to the apartment and joined the cocktail party, which already was well underway. Some groups were standing in open spaces, glasses in hand, talking, while others moved about the apartment admiring the furnishings and view.

"Marutus, I know you can't remember all our names. I'm Sam Justin. May I ask you about that painting?"

"Sure, Sam. It is Farinelli, the great castrato."

"He sang at the San Carlo Opera?"

"Oh, yes. And went to their school. And sang all over Europe; he was very famous."

"I like his expression. And his clothes and stance. Looks like a man of great style."

"Indeed. He was lionized everywhere. An icon. Oh, except perhaps in London."

"You admire him?"

"Of course. He was a great artist. I have a curious memento of his here," he said and pointed to a glass box on the table below the painting.

"Oh? A straight razor?"

"Yes, the story is that it was the razor used to castrate him as an unwitting boy. When he got his first major fee as an adult singer, he paid an assassin to kill the village barber to which his father had taken him as a child, reportedly with some vague promise of singing for the pope."

"Do you mean that this is the very razor with which he was castrated?"

"Reputedly. He took it with him everywhere in this box and had it in his dressing room at every performance. He called it, 'The Singing Razor.'"

"Marutus, the razor makes me nauseous."

"But imagine what it did to that child. He never sang for a pope and walked out on any performance if even a cardinal was said to be in the audience. Even in old age, he never entered a church and spat on the priest who tried to give him last rites. However, during his prime he was a great singer, an impeccable host, and a prize catch for top salons because of his wit, erudition, and fame."

Two Prime Numbers in the living room had squeezed in behind a small couch to examine an almost life-sized gilded Buddha on a table against the wall.

"Thai, I'd say. Look at the costume. Very beautifully done."

"Maybe it's a Thai dancer in a Buddha pose. Isn't that a dancer's head dress?"

"Maybe you're right. Wanna ask Marutus?"

"I'd rather ask you about something else, Jim. You're a big man in human genetics at that lab in San Diego. Can I ask you a question involving something in your field?"

"Yes, yes, don't make me sound so unapproachable."

"Do you think that homosexuality is genetic?"

"There's a lot of work still to be done, but yes, I do."

"We all know about the people who deny that, maintaining that it is simply a choice. Are they wrong?"

"Yes, they are mistaken."

"So, if they convince their gay sons that it will be possible to reject their gay sexual leanings by transferring them to women, they are mistaken?"

"Genetics cannot be changed this way. They are correct that they can turn their sons into closet queens, married with children, the whole thing."

"So, the homosexuality remains, we all know about that. Look at how many of our members here have children because of having had elders with that attitude."

"Quite a few Prime Numbers are fathers."

"They have contributed their genes to the human gene pool."

"Obviously."

"And in this way, actually furthered homosexuality."

"Very likely. What you are speculating about would have to be studied to be proven."

"Then can we say that anyone urging young homosexual men to marry and have children actually is fostering the incidence of homosexuality?"

"It is obvious what you are getting at. The answer is yes, they defeat their own purpose if that purpose is to discourage homosexuality."

"Thanks, Jim. Very interesting. That's what I'd hoped you would say."

"But you are talking about motivation. These are largely ignorant, uneducated people, socially in denial about something so simple. Their purposes would probably not be so grand. They might simply crave grandchildren or be grandstanding or be some number on television bent on lining his pockets through a bogus fundraising scheme."

"Yes, yes, whatever. But they at least incidentally increase the incidence of homosexuality by getting more gay genes into the pool."

"Very likely. Look, can we talk about something else? I came on this trip partly to get away from shop talk."

Out on a balcony, another two Prime Numbers were admiring the city lights when one of them said, "I eat pussy, you know."

"Darling," the other replied, "why do you make these abrupt pronouncements? Save them for confession."

"I just thought you might like to know."

"What I do know is that you haven't been close to a bare pussy in several decades. Every one of your friends knows about your early marriage, your two sons, your coming out at age thirty. Everyone here forgives you for having been so slow, so stupid really that you let yourself get trapped like that. No one cares that you ate pussy back then. Tell it to your confessor and make him gag. Lay off your friends."

And on the other side of the living room:

"Mark, I swear that this gold ceramic box must be a Sascha Brastoff. May I turn it over?"

"I think that would be all right. Go ahead."

"Yes, there is his name. A treasure. How do you suppose that it came to be here?"

"Well, Marutus did tell me that William Haines decorated the apartment for his aunt, so perhaps ..."

"Oh, well, if it was William then of course there would be something by Sascha. But where is Haines' signature moderne furniture?"

"Maybe the aunt didn't like it. He didn't always use it, you know. Ask Marutus, if you can find a moment with him."

At that moment, Marutus was being asked about something else.

"Marutus, how would the Prime Numbers be described in Italy?"

"Oh, that is easy. You are a confraternity. Here you might be called the Confraternity of the Prime Numbers."

"I like it. Maybe we can use it. We have been looking for something more descriptive but on the loopy side. Maybe a little formality is the way to go instead. The Melbourne Wankers really have topped the zippy category of names. Yes, confraternity might do. I will propose it when we get back to Palm Springs."

And two Prime Numbers talking on a balcony over the sea about the problems which one of them had. Marriage, with children.

"Heterosexual monogamy is much over-rated. What could be more disastrous for your psyche than having your very own multiparous little woman at home slaving over her hot microwave to produce a perfect Mrs. Miniver dinner for you? With candles. Every night."

"Try weekends at the zoo with the children. A new crisis every five minutes."

"Yes, all part of the same package. Why do you put up with it?"

"Well, the children, I suppose. But you're saying it all is undesirable?"

"Bingo. The cigar for this gentleman. Herman, life can be an endless run of meaningful one-night relationships with men if that is what you want."

"Well, but the children? We had those even though I used condoms every time."

"Ah, not enough to use them, darling, you have to store them in a maximum security safe. While you were at work, your mother-in-law was pushing needles through the tips of them. Classic entrapment."

"But now? I do like Palm Springs, and I could make a living there. And after every visit, I have to go back to Connecticut and the straight world. I hate it. Hate it."

"Now? Get a top divorce lawyer. Male. Secure some assets for yourself. Then a quick, clean divorce and move out. Take a second job if you have to so that you can send child support payments for the next ten years. Move to Palm Springs. See what good advice Daddy gives you?"

Two of the Prime Numbers, one a devout Bible historian, the other a firm atheist, often bantered with one another about their respective differences. Standing in one of the hallways, they quietly talked.

"I have a question for you Christians, but first a comment."

"Let's have the first."

"I think that they made it all up as they went along. It may have taken a couple of centuries of nattering bishops going at it in their councils, but I think they just made it all up."

"Yes, I understand. What would you ask them?"

"They finally worked out an easy, straight-line theory: creation on through some final destruction and resurrection, yes?"

"I'd agree with that. Is that the question you would like to ask them if it were possible?"

"No, my question is simpler than that."

"And it is?"

"And then what, boys?"

And other chatter and banter, the usual things, until finally it was time. "Who can compete with his fantasies?" "It was only a sentimental rape." "Socially, masochists are such weasels." "You know, Art Nouveau, the Paris dyke art movement, all those labial folds." "Yes, of course I like opera too, the music, the staging, the personalities. It's civilized and sophisticated. But, love, what does much of it mean? Tell me what that diva playing Aphrodite means when she bursts so joyously into her aria that begins 'The winds of heaven betray a fecund rancor.' What?!" "He was so fiercely hermetic." "Yes, an uncultured pearl." "And insufferably didactic." "Plus intolerably officious."

"Time, gentlemen," announced Mark. "Dinner. Say your thank yous, but if you miss them, maybe later. Marutus is going to dinner with us. This way out."

* * *

"Ethel, baby," said Hank with a growl. "You're really something."

"Aw, Hank. You're just saying that."

* * *

To jaded travelers and snobs with supercilious mind-sets, the little harbor of Santa Lucia on the urban seacoast of the city of Naples might seem to be a boring cliché to be avoided at all costs. In fact, its famousness is based on an incredible loveliness because of the setting. Everyone goes to see it. Neapolitans crowd there day and night. The restaurants lining the pleasure craft marina that now occupies the harbor delight thousands. The looming Castel dell'Ovo, which is on an island anchoring a short causeway forming one side of the harbor, is an ancient but utilitarian city building, in some respects the very symbol of Naples. The causeway is lined on the harbor side with popular restaurants.

It was here that the Prime Numbers came after Marutus' cocktail party for dinner, to a restaurant on the edge of the marina. Their single long table was set outside on the seawall, right beside the boats and docks. There were lights and music and activity and moonlight and quite good food, in several courses. Waiters in black bustled from kitchen to table, and everyone was served with professionalism and friendliness. Pleasant indeed, even wonderful, as several of the Prime Numbers remarked.

When at last the platters of fresh and dried fruit of the dessert course had been removed and dinner was over except for the few men finishing coffee, Mark reached over to William and held out a credit card discreetly below table level.

William shook his head no with a smile.

"The check," Mark murmured to him. "It is time to pay the piper."

William repeated his head shake, put his hand before his mouth, leaned over, and said in Mark's ear, "Comped."

Mark opened both eyes wide, raised his eyebrows in amazement, and whispered, "No. For thirty? Who?"

"Don't worry about it," William continued. "Wait. There's more."

William stood, raised a hand, cleared his throat, waited a moment for attention and silence from the long table, and made a brief announcement loudly enough so that everyone heard him.

"And now we have a special surprise. Our friend Marutus here has a new boy toy he would like to show to us. So we will go to see it in this little flotilla of skiffs just now coming up to the dock."

Chairs scraped against the cement floor, everyone stood, William said, "This way," briefly put his arm around Marutus' shoulders and squeezed, and they all walked, chattering, to the adjacent dock. There they gingerly boarded the rocking skiffs, put-putted off to an outer, heavily guarded part of the marina, and disembarked onto another dock. Marutus and a crewman then helped them one at a time aboard the stern of his new boat.

For thousands of years, Mediterranean peoples have gone down to the sea to board boat and ship, a continuous tradition. Here in the moonlight of the Bay of Naples, this simple procedure was being repeated. The boat was a new Navali di Roma model named *Itama*, a forty-six-foot-long blue beauty with a fiberglass hull, teak woodwork, two bedrooms, two baths, a large open midship area for passengers to loll about in, and a slightly raised bridge fronted by an enormous glass windshield. It looked like a greatly oversized speedboat, which was exactly what it was.

The Prime Numbers gathered mostly in the unroofed midship and also took turns looking through the cabins. William motioned to Mark, lifted a hatch cover near the stern, turned on a light inside, and they both climbed down a metal ladder into a spotless (not a drop of oil on the floor) room the width of the boat. The room contained only two identical objects, one on each side: great, 650-horsepower, baby blue, Mercedes diesel engines, glistening and still.

"Oh, shit!" expostulated Mark, with a delighted laugh. "It's like a gallery installation. What an engine room."

At that moment, both engines shuddered and roared to life. William covered his ears, then pointed toward the ladder, and he and Mark climbed back to the deck, carefully closing the hatch cover behind them just as the big boat pulled slowly away from the dock. A crewman near them coiled the mooring lines neatly, and Marutus stood at the wheel.

Carl came over to Mark and excitedly shouted above the roar of the engines, "Marutus says that we are making a run out and around Capri."

The boat then slowly moved from the marina to open water, the engine roar and vibration increased, and with a thrust that staggered the passengers and created instant wind, it leapt forward, white waves appeared midship, and a boiling wake trailed as it headed dead on for the lights on Capri. The wind smelled of the sea as only the wind on the open sea can smell at midnight.

From the street on the rise above the shore overlooking the marina, the fat man watched with a nod of approval as the boat moved straight up the shining path of the full moon.

V. THE RIDE TO THE ABYSS

"Unanticipated projectile vomiting."

"What?"

A short distance from Cape Misenum, at Cuma, the Greeks built an acropolis, which the Romans later enlarged. Today it is a ruinous archaeological site. Mark and the Prime Numbers visited this site and then walked downhill to the parking lot where the bus had been left. They crossed the lot to a nearby path leading to the Cave of the Sibyl. Bob and Henry were talking about Henry's cochlear implant, a device implanted in his skull that sent electrical impulses to the hair cells in his cochlea from a computer on his belt and a microphone hooked over his ear. Prior to the operation, Henry had been 100 percent deaf.

"Unanticipated projectile vomiting. That's what my doctor said would be the first symptom."

"Charming. I can just envision that. The metal in your new machine reacts with the tissues inside your head and forms a—what did you call it?—toxic hydroxyl, which causes meningitis. Then you vomit?"

"Well, that's what he said when I asked how I would know if the hydroxyl had formed."

"Then what? They remove the implant?"

"I don't think that they have time to bother with that. Then you just die."

"You die. And you let them drill a hole in your skull and put this thing permanently in your head?"

"Yes, but the chances of the hydroxyl forming are very low. And profound deafness really is the pits. I had resigned myself to becoming a little gray deaf man in the attic of some depressing retirement home in Hemet, California. Now here I am in Italy, listening to you, and having quite an ordinary conversation."

"Unanticipated projectile vomiting is not part of my ordinary vocabulary, much less my ordinary conversation. But I get it. You know, your hearing does seem normal to me except for the external machinery on your head, especially that big magnet. You feel self-conscious about that?"

"I had anticipated feeling as conspicuous as a walking Noraad station, with little children pointing to my head on the street. However, I finally realized that the real problem was vanity, and I decided simply to kill my vanity."

"Umm, Henry, you're amazing. How did you go about killing your vanity?"

"I traded in my Bentley for a Ford Focus. Everything else followed. It works. Try it."

* * *

Bob and Henry continued talking as they walked with the other Prime Numbers along the path. Finally, Mark stopped at the entrance to the Cave of the Sibyl, and they all gathered around for his introduction. The cave actually was a tunnel cut into volcanic ash on the side of the ridge on which the acropolis was built. They were standing at the ruined beginning of this cave.

"A word, friends, about what we are about to explore," he began. "This very curious structure is known as the Cave of the Sibyl, a cult, with a woman—the Sibyl—who uttered prophetic predictions. Is that a redundancy? Pardon. Anyway, this Sybil was one of several who were very famous in the ancient world, and there are numerous mentions of her in the surviving Greek and Roman texts. In actuality, it was a business. They charged very highly for the service. Like the ruins of the acropolis above, the tunnel may be as old as the seventh century B.C.

"It is about four hundred twenty-five feet long and in cross section is very curious. The shape here at the entrance extends all the way to the end. Note the flat ceiling, the walls below it that slope outwards, then this odd notch. Below the notch, the walls are vertical to the horizontal floor. There are regularly spaced side openings opposite one another that let in light.

"If this was made of building stones rather than being cut into solid rock, then the outline would be similar to the strange so-called arch used in several Mayan temples of southern Mexico and Guatemala. I know of nothing identical in shape in ruins of the Mediterranean area, although some of the water cistern tunnels in this very area have slightly similar outward sloping upper walls.

"It is very likely that this tunnel had doors, draperies, and furnishings, and perhaps even an entire wooden structure lining the interior, all missing now. How the structure functioned architecturally is unknown. It is this intriguing concept that I hope you will play with, you designers and architects. Give it a whirl and let's see what you might come up with.

"Any questions before we go in? Yes, Harry?"

"What kind of stone is the hill?" Harry asked.

"Carl, you're our geologist. Take this," Mark replied.

Carl moved over beside Mark and began, "This is the same kind of volcanic rock that we have been seeing all around Naples. It is a welded tuff, an airfall ash blown out of a volcano that still was hot enough when it came down so that the individual grains melted into one another and formed a solid mass. Many of the buildings in the Naples region are built of cut blocks of this kind of stone."

Fred, standing beside Harry, suddenly interrupted. "Wait a minute, Carl. If this tunnel might have been built as early as the seventh century B.C., then it already was here when Pliny the Younger watched Vesuvius erupt in 79 A.D. from Point Misenum, which is just over that way a few miles. That means that volcanoes were erupting around here for a longer time than I had understood."

Carl cleared his throat and glanced at Mark. "I think that Mark wants us to concentrate on the Cave of the Sybil, but I would like to answer that. Some of the volcanic sediments near here are very ancient, as much as forty-five thousand years old. The great event in our immediate area occurred thirty-five thousand years ago, an explosion of such a magnitude that it ejected enough ash and rock to empty the magma chamber below ground. This caused the land above it to collapse into the empty chamber, forming an enormous circular depression at the surface. We are near the center of that depression. Such a volcanic sinkhole is called a caldera by geologists. Remember that word—caldera."

There was a little buzz of interested chatter among the listeners and Fred asked another question.

"Like a limestone sinkhole, one formed when a cave roof in Florida collapses?"

"Exactly," continued Carl. "But in this case vast. This caldera is more than three miles wide."

Duke had a question too. "So the roof just collapses in a huge jumble?"

"It weakens and cracks into great blocks first, and then they all go down."

Duke continued, "Straight down?"

"Straight down, little jumble. Each block just goes straight down. If you've ever been to Crater Lake in Oregon, which occupies a caldera, think of the walls surrounding it. They are vertical fault scarps, indicating straight down."

Duke asked again, "How far down?"

"Maybe a mile."

Now Harry asked another question. "Do you mean to tell us that anyone standing here on the ground at that time would have dropped straight down for a mile? My god, what a thought."

Carl looked apprehensively at Mark, who nodded for him to proceed. "Yes, but the heat and fumes from the eruption would have killed him long before, and only his dead body would go down. In this area, though, when the caldera formed, the sea rushed in first and since then has been replaced partly by land. Some of the old caldera still is filled by the sea."

One of the men near Carl said to him, "Your caldera description made me think of the part of Faust, the Berlioz Faust, called *Ride to the Abyss.* It always makes the hair on the back of my neck stand up."

"Very interesting," interrupted Mark. "Thank you, Carl. Men, we are here to look at the Cave of the Sibyl. Let's all go in. When we come out, I want to hear your thoughts."

And so they all went inside, quite enthusiastically examining the place from one end to the other, the shape, the little holes that must have held supports for superstructure, the solidity of the very end of the tunnel, a great smooth wall that sounded hollow when pounded.

* * *

"Well?" asked Hank, looking up from the day old *Herald Tribune* he had been reading when Jane let herself into his cabin.

"Got it. Why are pursers on this shipping line always such pushovers?"

They both sat down in chairs before a little table and Hank took a printout sheet, which she handed him. He tapped briefly into his laptop computer as they watched the screen.

"Loaded," she remarked when a page came up. "And all apparently with the same bank, unless she has other accounts with a brokerage. We would be very comfortable for a while in Mar del Plata with that. Where is the dear lady now?"

"Her cabin. Nap time."

Jane stood, straightened her skirt, and peered closely into a mirror at her lipstick.

"I will go rouse our Ethel and take her to a late sisterly lunch. See what else you can find. She is perfect for us: a slow-witted, well-off, middle-aged woman. Ta ta, brother dearest."

She kissed him lightly on the cheek and left the cabin, and he returned to the computer.

* * *

Frank Bones opened the lobby door of his condo building and nodded to two workmen standing outside at the curb in front of motorcycles. They picked up leather bags with wooden hammer ends protruding from the tops and went inside while he held the door for them. In his free hand, Bones grasped two bunches of flowers about which neither man commented.

Once inside, he led them beyond the elevator doors to the adjacent stairwell where they walked down. Two floors down. Most of the lower stairwell was cut into the stone underlying the building foundation. At a very old and very thick iron door, Bones took out a heavy key, fitted it into the lock, turned it, and pulled the door open, accompanied by piercing squeals from rusted hinges and a rush of cold and moldy air that came up. He snapped on a large flashlight, stepped inside with the men, closed and locked the door behind them, and the three of them descended another two floors, opened a second similar door, and entered a large room with the ceiling hidden in shadow and in which the only features other than the bare floor, walls, and ceiling were two identical crypt spaces cut into the wall of the far side of the room, both at the same level and each large enough for a single prone body.

While the workmen stood respectfully to one side, Bones inspected their work from the previous week on each crypt by running his hands slowly and carefully over all five walls of each one. Then, he placed one hand on a slight protrusion and motioned for the workmen, who came to him with mallets, chisels, and files, and quickly smoothed it away.

Bones then put one bouquet in each crypt, the newly opened purplish caper blossoms bobbing in the flashlight beam. Each worker nodded approval, and they then all left the room, ascended the stairs, locking the lower and upper iron doors behind them, and returned to the main entrance of the building, where Bones handed each man an identical bundle of euros. He then shook hands with them while looking each straight in the eye, let them outside, watched as they very properly mounted their motorcycles, roared down the street, and disappeared into Spaccanapoli traffic.

Not a word had been spoken.

* * *

"William, love, here is a proposal to mull over. After this costume party, you effectively will have finished the volunteer work for your Prime Numbers group. Instead of continuing with them on the second leg of this trip to Stromboli and Taormina, come away with me for a few days to a favorite place in Ravello and let us consider the feasibility of you moving with your business to Naples and us living together here permanently. I cannot leave the opera; you can work anywhere. There are dozens of rich real and faux aristocrats and royals, retired ambassadors, ex-pats from many countries, and god knows camorra dons here and nearby who would keep your company humming with their events on estates, in palaces, on yachts, on private islands, the works. It would just be serious talk, a few quiet days for the two of us. Afterward I will go with you to the airport at Palermo to catch your flight home with the boys.

"No, don't tell me now. Think about it at least overnight."

* * *

The Prime Numbers had been through the Cave of the Sibyl, and now many of them were back at the entrance with Mark. It had not been quite the success for which he had hoped; there was more boredom than he had expected. The obviously uninterested men were straggling back toward the bus in the nearby parking lot or standing about in twos and threes discussing other things. Still, Mark had more than a dozen of them around him who wanted to talk about the cave.

"Well, Howard, you're our architect. What do you think?" he asked.

"Difficult, you know. This is one odd place. I can think of several possibilities, but none quite fits."

"For example?" Mark encouraged him.

"Well, for one, that curious cross-sectional outline that runs the length of the interior might have been a continuation of an outside building or a facade, now gone. Some of the tunnel entrance has collapsed. Look at that block there. I wonder if anyone has carefully searched downhill in this wood to see if some stones—if it was stone—from it still might be there. Perhaps stones from a collapsed facade were simply pushed over the edge and downhill to get them out of the way. Could it be reconstructed from them? There is much work to be done here still, basic exploratory work. It must be lack of money that has prevented it."

"And James," Mark turned to another man, "James, you've had some experience. Opinions?"

"I have no idea about a façade, but I did keep thinking about the repetition of the side bays. You assumed that they were just for light and ventilation, but I wonder. Suppose that each one was a separate and identical room, a tiny sleeping cell of some kind for the eunuchs, the priests and priestesses, the temple whores, or whomever and that there was a long central hall that had no other function except to lead to these. After all, the Romans and maybe the Greeks too had such tiny bedrooms. Look at the ones we still see in Pompeii and Herculaneum."

"Mark," said Fred, "I had the thought that the temperatures inside might stay rather uniform because of the bedrock. Cool in summer and not cold in winter if the bays were closed off properly at night and opened to the sun during the days."

"Interesting, Fred. Anything else?"

"Yes. This whole place would make one heck of an elegant shop, like that old place on Twenty-Sixth Street at San Vicente Boulevard in Santa Monica. But of course, it is larger."

"Look," Mark continued, "I want us to continue to think about this. Meanwhile, there is something else. The copies of the Petronius book now called The Satyricon that I ordered through the Feltrinelli bookstore on Piazza del Martini came last evening, and I have put copies for each one of us on the seats in the bus while you all were inside here. As I said before, this is a very early novel, today it would be called a picaresque novel, first-century A.D., the characters are young and mostly gay, they were in this very area, and one of them—where is it, ah here, this page—a fictional wealthy freedman who lived somewhere around here says, 'And, you know, I once saw the Sibyl of Cuma in person. She was hanging in a bottle, and when the boys asked her, Sibyl, what do you want? She said, I want to die.' Perhaps this bottle or whatever it might have been was hanging here in our cave. Incidentally, Petronius, the author, died in 65 A.D., fourteen years before the Vesuvius eruption, so he was contemporary with both our Plinys, although Pliny the Younger would have been only about three years old at the time of Petronius' death."

George asked, "Why would the Sibyl want to die?"

"Well, the story goes that when she was young and beautiful, Apollo wanted to bed her, but she resisted him until he offered her anything she wanted as a price. She asked for a long life of as many years as there were grains of sand in a nearby pile. There were a thousand. He gave her that, but she neglected to ask for continuing youth, so that eventually she became an ancient hag. It is the older Sibyl that Michelangelo painted on the ceiling of the Sistine Chapel, quite a wonderful hag's face, and with an impressively muscular male arm, very Michelangelo. Most of the other paintings depicted her as a young woman, beautiful in whatever the style for beauty was in that period."

Howard spoke up again. "If what several of us thought, that the hollow sounding end wall blocks something beyond, a continuation, is true, then the whole cave we saw today would merely be an ornate passageway to that. Perhaps a fissure at the end with CO_2 volcanic gas rising that produced the visions in the Sibyl."

"Excellent," replied Mark. "A success here, after all. Now let's gather the other men and get back on the bus and move out. Thank you, all."

"Just one other thing," continued Howard. "I am haunted by a memory of an outline shape of a passageway through a building I once saw at Uxmal. It seems very similar to our tunnel to me in outline. I will look on the hotel computer when we get back."

* * *

"Yes. Good-bye. And thank you so much. I am honored." John put the old-fashioned phone back in its cradle and wrote something on a pad.

"Honey, who was that?" asked Mary, looking around the kitchen door into the living room.

"Oh, a command performance. It was the American ambassador. Apparently someone at the opera house business offices gossiped to the opera administration that I was here, and they called the American embassy, and now we are to attend a command performance."

"At the opera? How wonderful. But it is August. I thought they only had winter seasons."

"Yes, that's true. But this hot-shot new city mayor has arranged a special performance this month, the tourist month, to get tourists to the opera and drum up broader interest in it and also to raise funds for the opera foundation, badly in need of money. Apparently a United States senator is coming and a New York philanthropist too. But they still needed others for the VIP contingent and just heard that I was here. We will have to do it. More people will be bused from Rome, and there is a special train coming from Florence."

"I will have to buy us things to wear. Helen too. She will be so excited."

"No, she will have to stay home. We are to sit in the royal box with the bigwigs. Two seats. Adults only."

"Oh, well, she'll understand grown-ups only. Do you suppose the landlord has a tux you can use? You are about the same size."

"No, but he will know where we can buy one. We will ask. And a suitable long dress for you."

"Oh, John, I just remembered. Those boxes we shipped ahead and are still unopened in the garage. I may have included your tuxedo and a long dress for me just in case. I will go look now."

"Mary, I will tell Helen that her mother is brilliant. Give us a kiss. How long before Helen comes home?"

VI. TAKE OFF THE MASK

The little car, top down, raced along the *lungomare* en route to the opera house, the two occupants with hair whipping erratically about their heads and sunglasses shielding their eyes from the sun directly ahead and climbing above Vesuvius.

"Yes."

"Yes?"

"Yes about jumping ship and going with you to Ravello instead of to Stromboli and Taormina with the fellows."

Marutus threw back his head and whooped, sounded three toots on the car horn, pushed the gear shift forward, and roared ahead of the traffic.

"Excellent, babe. I will tell them this morning that we definitely are coming. I already know that they have a vacancy."

William wanted to lean over and buss him on the cheek but refrained because of propriety. Despite a few thousand years of same-sex relationships, Naples still had a lot of hang ups about it. Instead he laughed along with Marutus and squeezed his knee.

* * *

A hundred feet below the surface of the old part of Naples, the Prime Numbers were being escorted through a modest section of the many miles of tunnels, galleries, quarries, and rooms that underlie the entire city. Carl had told them that most of them were dug into the famous thick layer of yellow welded tuff, the volcanic ash that was so hot when it fell that the grains melted into one another, similar to the rock of the Cave of the Sibyl. Their main tour leaders here, however, were from a group called Underground Naples, which regularly ran tours through the safer areas, although they themselves famously explored the unknown tunnels and were adding information about them to a map begun in the nineteenth century. They now were in one of the larger tunnels that had electric lights along one wall. Guido, one of the Underground Naples men, spoke up.

"Prepare yourselves. We will now turn out the lights and then you can imagine what it might have been like for the people who were here long before electricity, a thousand years ago, two thousand years ago, perhaps even three thousand years ago."

At his signal, a switch was thrown, and the lights blinked out and were replaced by a darkness darker than any night, a heart of darkness. There was an amazed murmur and then a burst of applause.

A dozen tiny flames from lighters appeared and next were quickly replaced by larger flames that turned out to be sterno in containers embedded in the top ends of faux torches. The men who had lighted these now held them straight up at arm's length, illuminating the group in firelight against shadow. Next the torchbearers rapidly circled the Prime Numbers, causing shadows to dance against the walls. Guido spoke again.

"Light such as this but from real burning wooden torches was the chief illumination available to the people who built and used these tunnels. We also have found the kind of small oil lamps used by the Greeks and Romans. If these lights failed, tunnelers were left in darkness, sometimes unable to find a way out, and they died here. We have found skeletons of people who appear to have died like that."

"Mark," called George, "how long are we going to be in this kind of light? I am beginning to feel claustrophobic and nauseated."

"Behold," boomed Mark dramatically, "let there be light, Guido." The electric lights were turned on again and the torches extinguished.

"Yes," said Guido, "that happens to many people on our tours. You would have been an unhappy camper if you had been here when this was an air raid shelter in the 1940s." He paused, and then continued. "Now, we have seen an air raid shelter, a Nazi bunker, some quarries for building stones used in the city above, a garbage dump in a vertical tunnel, a Roman aqueduct, a Greek burial chamber, a Roman cemetery with pots for cremated remains, and now we will visit a catacomb, one of several ancient Christian burial areas in the complex."

They followed Guido down the enormous tunnel and then entered a side doorway that led into a series of rooms and all paused again once inside.

"This was a catacomb used by nuns of a now-defunct convent during the sixteenth and seventeenth centuries. It is similar to one still maintained, illegally of course, by present-day nuns elsewhere in the city. We broke through an old, sealed door a few years ago and discovered that one, causing the ladies a great fright."

Someone asked, "Well, how did this place function? What are these long niches, what is this odd stone chair, what are those shelves, and where were the bodies placed?"

"Yes," replied Guido, "a recently dead sister would have been bound in this stone chair until her body fluids had drained off, then lain on one of the shelves until the tendons disintegrated, and finally the skull and individual bones would have been put with other similar bones on the shelves in artistic arrangements."

"Oof, filthy women," commented someone else to himself but loudly enough so that others near him heard and laughed.

"Of course, all the bones found here have been removed to a cemetery on the surface."

"Guido," Mark asked, "I have just noticed that the stone chair has a hole in the center of the seat. Uh, don't tell me …"

"Yes," Guido said, with a laugh, "I do tell you. The ladies were neater than the monks who had similar burial chambers and had this hole cut to conduct the body fluids to a container below the seat."

He reached underneath and felt around, "Ah, yes, here it is," and brought out a small crock. "The monks had no such device, and the body fluids of the men just stained the whole chair and the floor around it in their catacombs."

"Ghouls," someone else snorted, "just like modern undertakers. I don't even want to think what such minds might have done with the contents of that crock."

And then they all filed through the catacomb doorway back to the main tunnel and started the trek up to the city above, mounting stairway after stairway.

"Hey, Mark," Harry said thoughtfully, "have you noticed how many of these tunnel walls slope inwards in their upper parts, something like the Cave of the Sibyl?"

"That," Guido interrupted, "is a structural feature intended to lessen the cave-ins that occur here all too often and wreck buildings at the surface and cause holes in the streets. It now is illegal to excavate anymore tunnels because of the danger."

"Ah," commented Mark, "maybe the Greeks knew this too, and the sloping walls of the Cave of the Sibyl were intended somehow to protect the heavy stone buildings of the acropolis above in a similar way. Anyway men," and he spoke more loudly, "now we go upstairs and out into the world of the living for lunch and then to sort through an incredible collection of old costumes at the San Carlo Opera for the ones we want to wear to our own costume party tonight. Everybody ready for that?"

There were a couple of cheers and some yeas, and they all continued up the stairway.

* * *

That is only a cat lying in the sun, thought John, looking up from the piano and out the French doors in a moment of frustration while working on his musical. *My heroine, usually so frenetic, needs a quiet moment on stage alone. I will say aloud what I want to have her sing plaintively, pensively, perhaps while holding a flower.*

"It's only a cat lying in the sun there. It's only a breeze blowing in from the sea there. I only will snip this loveliest rose here. It's all no matter to me."

Maybe I need a quiet interlude in my own life too. It's only the cat and the wind and the rose for me too, but do I still appreciate these things myself? Busy with this work and being a fucking family head too, trying to do the right things by a wife and a demanding child I never wanted. Nothing I do seems to matter beyond that. But today is the birthday of Augustus. I am in Naples, which still celebrates it with fireworks from barges on the bay. Augustus, riding his phallus-hung chariot pulled by white horses up the history road to the long-gone Temple of Jupiter on the Palatine summit, running down anyone and everyone who got in the way of his ambition, a psychic triumph we still dream of, Antony and Cleopatra among the many people crushed beneath his wheels, the slave behind him whispering repeatedly in his ear.

"Look behind you. Remember you are a man."

John walked to the patio, took the shears from a table, smelled the rose dancing in the wind and sun, and then cut it, took it to the kitchen, filled a vase with water, put the rose in it, and wrote a note to go under the vase.

"Mary, darling. I will be back tomorrow. All my love, John."

* * *

Professor Bones and his student assistant, Mario, each placed a pair of glass cups, the rubber suction devices used for attachment to large panes of glass so that they can be moved, on opposite ends of the wall case front inside the Naples Paleontology Museum, threw the levers that activated the suction, firmly grasped the handles, lifted the glass from the case, moved it to one side, and leaned it against an adjacent wall. The case front now was open. Bones took his tape measure and ran it along the vacant interior, calling out the dimensions for Mario to write on his note pad.

"Three meters by two meters by one meter. They do make it simple. Okay, let's get the glass back up."

They lifted and reinstalled the big glass front and were putting the glass cups in a box when Mario said, "Uh, sir, someone ..."

Bones turned, brushing the dust from his hands, to find a tall, redhead fellow standing close by at parade rest and looking at him.

"Mario, would you take these things back to my office and enter the dimensions into our computer program? I will see you there later."

As Mario disappeared around a bend in the gallery, the smiling redhead moved closer and spoke for the first time.

"So, this is Naples."

Bones simply stared at him for a long moment and then responded.

"Red, you have one chance. Go now or be doomed."

"No possibility. Leaving is not an option."

"Then the worst will come. Let us go off campus for coffee and you can present your proposal."

* * *

"Mom, it's Ethel ... No, no, no problems. I'm fine ... Well, I just wanted to talk with you ... Oh, the time. It's about five PM here. I knew you would be at home and getting dinner ready ... Yes, the ship has telephones they let you use ... That's nice. Thank you ... Yes, we saw a town called Naples and are on the way to some other ones, including one named Venice where they say the houses all are built on islands and everybody uses boats instead of cars to get around ... Yes, yes, I am fine. Fine ... He did? That's nice for you. I'm glad to hear it … Yes, but Mom, I want to tell you that I have met a very nice fellow … Oh, yes, on the boat. Yes, with the tour. His sister is here too. I had lunch with her today … No, they're Americans, both about my age. They live in Ohio … I think it was Cincinnati, but I'm not real sure … Well, I had a long talk with his sister this afternoon. She says that Hank might ask me to marry him … Well, that's his name, Hank. Her name is Jane …

"Mom? Mom? Please. Please … Well, I don't know when. He hasn't said anything at all yet. She just told me a little while ago … I don't know … I don't know … Mom I hope you won't do that. Why would you call the cruise line about him? … Mom … Mom … Don't say that. They're lovely people. You will like them … What I mean is that they will come to visit us in Des Moines after we get back … Mom, please don't shout like that. It's bad for your nerves. I can hear you. Why are you upset? …

"Yes, of course I will do something for you … A promise? … Not to marry him before you meet him? Mom, how could we do that? … Oh, the ship's captain could? But I don't think … Mom, please … Yes, of course, anything … What? His passport? Well, I suppose the ship office has it. They take up all the passports and give them back when we leave. But they tell us to make a copy to carry with us on trips off the boat. I suppose he keeps the copy in the safe in his cabin. They told us to do that when we first came aboard … Copy it? Copy Hank's passport? You mean like on a copying machine? … Well, yes, I suppose they must have a copying machine I could use.

"But Mom, why? … Yes, I understand. Every page he has in his copy. Especially his home address. I guess they would give me that easy enough … And then fax it to you? But Mom, even if I could get it without him knowing, I don't think I should. I'll just ask him for it … Mom. Please, Mom, please … Why should I keep it such a secret? … Oh, he wouldn't think it was nice … And you only want to know some real facts about him … But Mom, you said you might call the cruise line. Don't cause any trouble for me. This is such a lovely trip …

"Oh, if I fax you the copies, you won't call the cruise company … Well, if it really means so much to you, I suppose I could. I will try. I don't know why you want me to do this, Mom. It doesn't seem right … They are wonderful people. So nice, just lovely … Yes, Mom, thank you … I will. No, I won't forget. I think I can do it, but I don't like the idea at all … Yes, important to you … And keep it a secret … Okay, Mom. Nice to talk to you. You will like Hank and Jane … Yes, I am sure you will … I love you, Mom … Yes, me too … Bye, Mom."

* * *

With a hand-held steamer borrowed from their landlord, Mary was removing wrinkles from the clothes that she and John would wear to the opera. There was a classic tuxedo for him and a black silk dress with spaghetti straps for her, to be worn with an authentic nineteenth-century paisley shawl. Later she would touch up troublesome places with an iron. Helen, home from school a little early, was questioning Mary.

"Mommy, does the opera not have enough money? Is that it? Is that why they're having this special fundraising show tonight?"

"No, Helen, that's not it. Your father says that they have a very substantial endowment indeed but that the mayor wants to increase it by tapping wealthy American visitors and also some American politicians and foundations who will be here. This is a first, a trial balloon to see if it will work. The opera invests the endowment money and then spends only a percentage of the interest it earns so that they always have money. A good model for you to think about in your adult life. You can have your money and spend it too, over and over again. Just don't touch the principal."

"Like Grandpa?"

"Yes, like Grandpa and his trust. Although in his old age he's suddenly decided not to think about that rule any more, and he now does a lot of extravagant things that cause trouble."

"Why doesn't that steam burn the cloth?"

"Here, you hold it and try it. Just move it back and forth slowly so that the steam dampens the dress and causes the wrinkles to disappear. Steam isn't hot enough to burn the cloth. I guess you haven't learned that in school yet."

"We learned that steam was two hundred twelve degrees Fahrenheit, but I don't know how hot that is."

"Well, it isn't hot enough to burn this tuxedo if you iron properly. Now move it up around the lapels. See how those folding creases just fall out?"

"If I did burn it, would Daddy have to stay home?"

"Helen, give me the steamer. Don't even think about such a thing."

"Why? Would Daddy be mad?"

"Helen, we depend on the money your daddy brings home from his work so that we can live and travel this way and you can go to such good schools. You have to think about how you can help make it easier for him now that you are growing up."

"A child's responsibility to its parents. Miss DeRosa told us about that."

"Whatever she said is probably true. You must help your daddy and me in every way you can. We depend on you to do that now."

"Oh, yeah, Mommy. I'll be very good. You'll see."

"I hope so, dear. Now you get ready too. Our neighbors will be here very soon to take you for your sleepover. Won't that be fun?"

"Maybe. I don't like Diana's brother."

"You will be very careful, a perfect little guest, so that your father and I will be proud of you."

"Where was Daddy last night? He wasn't here for breakfast."

"I don't know where he was, dear. Sometimes he has to get away to clear his head so that he can work better."

"Don't you mind?"

"I don't mind anything that helps him with his work. Now you go change clothes and be quiet so you don't wake your father."

* * *

At a wine bar just outside the University of Naples, Bones ordered two coffees and, when they were put on the counter, handed one to Red.

"What kind of coffee is this?"

"Turkish coffee. Especially strong. Good for your jet lag."

They took the tiny cups, walked around the groups of people standing and talking, found a quiet table, and sat down facing one another.

"Tell me how you found me."

"Your friend Eugene said that you had gone to Chicago. I doubted that, and then he told me it was a neighborhood in Chicago named Spaccanapoli. It was all downhill from there. One call to the university here. Easy."

"And you're at the Grand Hotel Parker's?"

"How did you know that?"

"I have my sources too. What's it like?"

"Like an American Ritz-Carlton. The men are rich and the women sincere, as they say."

They both sipped the sweet, syrupy coffee, and then Bones spoke again.

"Okay, let's have it."

"I have come to ask if we could be friends again. We both did far-out things, I know, but now we're even."

"So, you're in love with me? San Francisco to Naples is a long way to ask about a friendship."

"I think so."

"Love, you do know, is purely biochemical, almost like cupid's arrows. A colleague at Berkeley in the chemistry department says it has been isolated."

"Someone will be rich."

"He's a romantic humanitarian too. After realizing what the knowledge would do to civilization, they destroyed the formula."

"Nevertheless."

"Yes, nevertheless, there it is. You have this problem. I expected it. And you. What do you want to do about it?"

"I have bought a big, painted lady, Victorian house in San Francisco, quite a wonderful house, four stories, right on Buena Vista Park. Next year when you come back from this sabbatical, I want you to come live with me in it."

"Two married gays. Elegant dinner parties for friends. Expensive vacations to exclusive places. Weekends in Mendocino. Season opera tickets. The best cars, in one of which I commute to Berkeley. Is that it?"

"Close enough."

"Your mother give you the money for the house?"

"Yes."

"You tell her why?"

"Not exactly."

"She will know why. She wants her gay little boy to bring a partner home to see her and then settle down with him. Did she mention grandchildren?"

"No."

"She will. She wants the whole thing."

"Bones, you really don't know my mother well. And this is about you and me."

"Listen, when you were a tiny baby, she and I walked into your nursery one day and found you fishing into your diapers, grabbing handfuls of your own shit, and cramming them into your mouth. Know what your loving mother said?"

"No."

"Your adoring mother said 'Oh, dear, now I will have to get him to a therapist.' Six months old and she made an appointment for you with a therapist."

"I don't believe that."

"It's true. What you believe is irrelevant."

"Anyway, what's your reaction? It would be very stylish and comfortable."

"I do not want stylish and comfortable."

"And the sex would be Class A."

"You cannot give me what I need sexually, ever."

"And that is?"

"Furtive anonymity."

"We could play delivery man."

"I need the real thing."

"Will you think about it?"

"No."

"Will you see me again while I'm here?"

"Yes. I will pick you up at your hotel tomorrow night at nine. Be ready to go out to dinner."

They both stood, shook hands, and left the wine bar in separate directions, Red whistling a phrase from *Scheherazade*, "Entry of the Golden Slave."

* * *

Harry and George did the Macarena in the aisle as the sound system played Gilbert and Sullivan pieces and the bus moved slowly through the traffic.

"Scugnizzi alert," someone shouted and knocked on the closed bus window as they passed three young men in the sidewalk crowd, one of whom turned, grabbed his balls in the evil-eye-averting gesture, and then pointed to the single English word printed front and center on the chest of his knock-off Dolce & Gabbana T-shirt.: LUNCH.

The whole bus sang along as they drove on and then were waved by a guard into a special parking space beside the San Carlo Opera house.

"Pert as schoolgirls well can be, Filled to the brim with girlish glee, Three little maids from school."

Mark ejected the CD and picked up the microphone as the driver turned off the engine.

"Awww," went up from the Prime Numbers.

"Great giddy-up start to party time, men. Save some energy for later. It might be a bumpy ride tonight. Now, William and Marutus have arranged for us to use vintage costumes for tonight's party here. We will go in, look through the racks of available ones, write our names on the paper tags for the ones we want to wear, and then go back to the hotel for some quiet time. Try on the costumes if you wish to make sure of the fit. Don't rush but don't dawdle either, please. Questions."

"What about makeup?"

"William says that there will be plenty of stage makeup here for you tonight, including all kinds of greasepaint. But please bring any you have and perhaps share it. I expect that Marilyn Monroe blue eye shadow would be appreciated. And mink eyelashes. And quality pirate moustaches."

"Don't we take the costumes back to the hotel with us?"

"No, we come back here later to change and then change again after the party and leave the costumes here. There will be locked lockers for our clothes, but don't bring too much cash, just in case."

The driver, who understood only Italian, grinned and pulled the door handle at Mark's nod and the door opened.

"Let's go," said Mark cheerfully.

* * *

"John, dear," said Mary, shaking him gently by the shoulder. "Oh," he said, "what time is it?"

"Early, but I thought if you got up now, then we wouldn't be rushed later."

He stretched, reached out, and pulled her down on the bed with him.

"Are you sure that's what you were thinking? Where's Helen?"

"She already has gone to her slumber party. And you really should get up, you know."

"Aw, Mary, you're pissed because I stayed out."

"No, I am not. Well, yes, I am a little. Where were you all night?"

"First, I walked all the way down to the bay, had a long, quiet drink in one of those jerry-built bars, waited until the sun went down, and then watched the fireworks. Could you see them?"

"Yes, what were they?"

"Oh, it's August, the month named for the Roman emperor Augustus. They celebrate his birthday with fireworks every year."

"Still? You mean the real Augustus, the one related to Julius Caesar?"

"Yes, yes, yes. It's Italy, after all. He was a great man."

"And then what did you do?"

"Nosy."

"No, I mean, really, where did you spend the whole night?"

"Well, I went back to our studio in the opera house building and worked out an entire scene, the one I was having such trouble with."

"And you slept in the studio?"

"Yes, surprisingly comfortably. You remember the bench with the cushions? On that. A little adventure. An innocent adventure."

"They let you in and then let you stay there too, outside of our scheduled time and all night?"

"That was a funny thing, Mary. The building was open, the lights were on, but there wasn't anybody there. Nobody at that high desk at the end of the hall where we usually sign in, nobody around at all apparently."

"No wonder you slept all afternoon here."

"I slept there too though. Had an odd dream about a big fat man coming in the door and telling me something that seemed awfully important at the time, but now I can't remember what it was at all."

* * *

Ethel smiled at her friends and then said, "Sweet Jane and dear Hank, this has been such a lovely dinner with you. Thank you for asking me. We will be in another port tomorrow, and I hope you will let me take you both out there."

"Ethel," replied Jane, "you are too kind. We would love that, wouldn't we Hank?"

"Unh, yes, you bet," responded Hank. "It may have to be lunch if it is going to be ashore because I heard that we sail early from the next port."

"Oh, here's our coffee," continued Ethel as the waiter came with three cups on a cart. "And I brought these sweets to go with it."

"My, Ethel, what a pretty box," said Jane. "What are the candies?"

"Marzipan they told me. Have one please, Jane. You too, Hank."

"Interesting," commented Jane after her first taste. "And nice, very nice. But an odd flavor for marzipan. Something a little tart was added, almost bitter. Did you buy these on the ship?"

Ethel took another bite and then answered. "No, but maybe one of the onboard shops has them if you want some. We could ask around. I got these at the ship terminal in Naples just before we sailed. They were being sold by the loveliest nuns, and I think they said they made them."

* * *

And now, here they are, the Prime Numbers of the Desert, from culture-deprived, cachet-lacking little Palm Springs, California, in the bowels of the venerable San Carlo Opera in Naples, Italy, face to face with a handsome youngish man who looked uncomprehendingly at Mark, their spokesman, when he said:

"Hello, I'm Mark. We're here to look at some costumes that Marutus and William told us about."

Assistants swarmed about, picking up armfuls of clothing and pushing racks and bins of costumes out the door, down the hall, and into an elevator. The Prime Numbers stood quietly, waiting for development.

At that moment, William came hurrying down the hall and said, "Mark, how nice to see you here. Things are a little chaotic right now. Excuse it, please. The racks in the next room have the costumes for our party. Through here, please."

And he and Mark strode into the room, the Prime Numbers following, to find several portable racks laden with bright opera and ballet costumes on hangers.

"Help yourselves, please," Mark began. "Write your names on the tags for the ones you wish to use and transfer them to the empty racks over there. I will lock the door when you leave so that no one disturbs them. There are ballet as well as opera costumes, but we do not have any dance belts so you will have to be disgraceful, or thrilling, depending on your endowment and viewpoint, if you choose one with tights, but who will care? Can you just get started? This is Giuseppe, the wardrobe master. He will help you with everything. Please speak Italian to him or ask someone who does if you wish to talk to him."

"Got it," Harry suddenly said. "I knew you were familiar but couldn't place the face. Giuseppe Salvatore. I saw you dance in Havana three years ago. Divine, just superb. The audience was in tears at the beauty of it. You were sensational."

Mark translated to the now-beaming Giuseppe, who knew a fan when he saw one and who instantly picked a costume off the rack and held it against Harry to gauge the fit.

"Hmmm?" he asked.

"I'll take it," said Harry with a big smile.

Just then, Marutus came in and said, "Oh, good, you're here. Everything going okay, I hope. Please excuse the hubbub. We are damnably busy this afternoon."

"Yes, we're on schedule," replied William. "We can handle it now. We'll be okay."

Marutus smiled. "Sure. Find me if you need help." He raised a hand in farewell and left. Already the Prime Numbers were rummaging through the costumes, reading the tags and assessing size, cut, color, and style.

"Look, Iago, 1875," exclaimed one. "God, what a thrill if this would fit me."

"And the Black Swan," said slim George. "My gorgeous saber legs would look great under this tutu. But are there toe shoes that would fit?"

And other similar comments.

"Figaro, here."

"Oh, Othello."

"Attila."

"Super! Desdemona, a lifelong dream."

They lifted costumes from the racks, sat in nearby chairs, tried on shoes, stood and slipped on breeches, dresses, and wigs, and assessed the results in mirrors lining the walls. A new society was emerging.

Carl, who quickly had found a simple pageboy outfit that he liked, wandered back into the hall and then looked into a nearby stairwell, wondering where it led.

"Psst," sounded from above him and there, two stories up, leaning over a railing, was his friend the fat man, motioning for him to come up. When he got there, he was welcomed with a pat on the shoulder, led to a nearby room, and introduced to a thin woman who was seated at a table, sewing sequins onto an apparent costume.

"This is my sister, Judith, Carl."

"How do you do, Judith. I'm pleased to meet you."

"Same here," she replied, continuing to sew. "Enjoying Naples, are we, dear?"

"Yes, immensely. Odd, though, that so many people use exactly that phrase in asking. Any idea why?"

The fat man chuckled, his girth heaving. "Yes, it is a local joke, Carl. That is what doxy Emma Hamilton asked Admiral Horatio Nelson the first time she met him here. What did you do today, Carl?"

"Well, underground Naples first, then costumes downstairs here. Tonight the gay Naples people are coming to a party we're having outside in the very gardens you showed me the other day. This morning, I woke very early and went out for a walk. Talked to some men sitting on the rocks of the seaside breakwater."

The fat man and his sister glanced at one another.

"And who were they?" she asked.

"Very amusing guys. Older, you know. Learned English from the GIs who were here in the 1940s."

"Carl, you do get around," commented the fat man. "Any feeling that they might have been dangerous?"

"No, I didn't think they were. Perhaps they were gay too. They joked that they were the original sirens of the sea here, luring sailors onto the rocks."

Now the sister giggled. "As a matter of fact, the original sirens were very straight and very female and real women indeed."

"And then, back to the hotel. It was still too early for breakfast, so I went to sleep and dreamed about your lady sirens. Very odd legs in my dream."

"Yellow, huh?" asked the sister.

"Yes, cadmium yellow. How did you know? And they sang a very strange song, unlike anything I ever even imagined."

"Something like this?" asked the sister, vocalizing.

"Yes, yes, quite like that. How did you know that?"

Just then, Mark's voice came up the stairwell. "Carl, Carl. Are you up there? We're leaving."

"Gotta run. Hope to see you both again."

"Yes, we do too," said the sister, slipping another sequin onto her needle, down the thread, and fastening it to the material with a mattress stitch. As she tied the knot, Carl was already at the foot of the stairs.

"Competent and attractive," Judith remarked to her brother, "Perhaps more. We will see."

"I have already decided."

VII. BOOGALOO

It was twilight on a warm August night in the garden that borders the back and one side of the San Carlo Opera. Guests were arriving for a party, some down the paths from the parking area at the far end of the adjacent Royal Palace, others through a basement door of the opera house itself. Everyone was in costume, anticipating a fun evening at the party being given jointly by the Prime Numbers from California and the ARCIGAY Naples men. In an area off the outside double stairway of the opera house, groups of them already had gathered, some at the makeshift bar, others at candlelit wooden tables and chairs, some standing at the foot of a temporary stage. There was a susurrus of underlying conversation broken by an occasional staccato laugh. Strings of paper lanterns strung between the trees swayed in a light breeze and then blinked as the electricity surged when the sound system was turned on. A Prime Number with a portable microphone walked on stage, tapped it, and blew into it twice.

"Testing, one, two, one, two, three, counting. Give me your tired, your old, your addled asses yearning to breathe free."

Someone in the crowd shouted, "Emma, you go girl."

"Your wretched refuse of your Rainbow Casket, send these, the homeless, tempest-tossed to me, I lift my lamp beside the golden door. Perfect; all set."

There was a scattering of applause and one whoop. He left the stage, and the small combo that had been setting up on one side of it began playing. A huge jacaranda tree dropped blue flowers on them like snow.

William and Mark, dressed in identical ephebe tunics and sandals, stood nearby, watching.

"William," said Mark, "you are doing a terrific job for us on this trip. The cocktail party, dinner, and boat trip around Capri the other night were unforgettable. And I expect that tonight will be wonderful too. Tell me, are great parties, the successful ones, just the result of meticulous planning?"

"There does have to be planning and preparation. It is work. It can be tedious, even frustrating to do. But there comes a moment near the beginning of the event itself when you just step away, leave it alone, and permit it to develop by itself. Micro-management will kill spontaneity and spoil a party. For example, the mother of the bride rushing around at a wedding reception, teeth gnashing, issuing corrective orders, will ruin it for everyone. Tonight, for example, I am through here. Everybody knows his job. This either will or won't take off. The great god Random Chance is in charge now."

"What was the greatest party ever, in your opinion?"

William thought a second, running his tongue around his lips, and then continued. "Probably the greatest party ever lasted a full year and was given by Antony and Cleopatra. They both deserted the battle of Actium and fled in her ship to Alexandria, built a pleasure pavilion on a point in the royal harbor, engaged the gay Greek party designer Apollodorus, invited entertaining friends, and partied while waiting for the Roman army to come kill them. Partied for a year. Lots of gays. The kitchen had meals going day and night so that they could be served anytime at a moment's notice. Very late on the last night, with the Roman army at the gates, everyone in the city heard a troupe of entertainers pass through and out into the desert. Supposedly this was Antony's personal party god, Bacchus, and his entourage leaving. Party over. Both Antony and Cleopatra died next day, and Alexandria and Egypt became Roman after almost three hundred years under the rule of the Greek Ptolomies."

Mark whistled. "Wow, a whole year. I never heard that. What a story. Of course, we can't expect anything legendary like that for our party tonight."

William looked at him and raised both eyebrows. "Mark, yes you can. I have seen some smashers grow from lesser potential than we have here. Nothing is impossible, especially with the institutions involved with this. At the very least, it should be great fun."

Almost all of the Prime Numbers now were out of the opera house basement in their costumes, moving about, being admired, posing, laughing. They mixed easily with the joyful gay Napoletani who wore equally exotic costumes, many of which they had worked on for years.

The stage footlights dimmed, then went out, the combo played, then black lights were turned on, and a young black man walked on stage with the microphone, nude except for a white top hat, white gloves, white tap shoes, and white spats, all of which glowed brilliant purple in the ultraviolet lights.

"Mercy," someone shouted.

The fellow tap danced to center stage and sang into the mike:

"Oh, oh, oh, oh,
Mmy ba-by doll,
Ooh, oh, oh, oh."

He then tapped the same beat, mixed tapping and singing the same words.

"Harry," asked George, "isn't that our friend Ahmadou from the Blu Angel Baths?"

"Oh, so it is. I thought he might find some way to merchandise that monster whopper flopper, but I never expected quite this. Wonder where his brothers are."

The combo merged into another melody, and the young man sang and tapped: "My sugar is so divine."

Giuseppe had come up with other costumes, and there now was a plethora of queens, including Maria Carolina, Carolina Bonaparte, Maria Christina, Marie Antoinette, and four Cleopatras. There were tiaras and trains, fur wraps, and rhinestone chokers. Among the males, there were two Murats, one in the Hussar uniform and the other in the outfit from the royal palace facade statue. Later these two won a joint Best of Party prize and separately the Most Splendid Ass and the Best Basket awards. The two Murats were so pleased that they danced a special waltz together on stage, laughing and taking turns leading, ostrich feathers on their helmets bobbing and rhinestones glittering.

Between sets, two fellows in togas and Greek comedy masks placed a simple column on one side of the stage, draped a long piece of purple linen over it, and propped a mask on top.

"William, what is that?"

"Carissimo, I have no idea. Remember what I told you about spontaneity?"

A young Napoletano dressed as Tiny Tim took the stage and sang in a shrill falsetto:

"Got along without you
Before I met you,
Gonna get along
Without you now."

Near the bar, a gallant in garter and silk hose asked a be-ribboned lady, "Emma Hamilton, is that ye?"

She replied, "Nay, nay, good sir. 'Tis not the Hamilton bitch but only I, the king's whore."

"Ah, of course, Nell Gwyn, not Emma at all."

"But close, ducks, close indeed."

The prosecco flowed into glass after glass after glass.

"And now," said the master of ceremonies into the microphone, "The Prime Numbers Quartet will sing a song from the Boy Scout Jamboree Songbook."

Four matronly ladies in four entirely different costumes took the stage, hummed a deep baritone chord, and launched into "The Mayor of Bayswater's Daughter."

The Mayor of Bayswater,

He had a pretty daughter,

And the hairs of her dinky-di-doo,

Hang down to her knees.

"John, friend, come sit by me. You are a well-known English lit prof. I have a question, a serious question. What is glamour? No examples, please, those are too easy."

"I won't give you an example, I will give you a demonstration. Hand me that blue eye shadow."

"Can't the glamour concept be applied to objects and places too?"

"Ah, I think I see where you're going. The city of Naples?"

"Yes. Is Naples glamourous?"

"Indeed it is. Perhaps a ruinous glamour, but it is there. However, that is a human interpretation, nothing inherent again."

"And things?"

"Yes, by association partly but also by contrived beauty. Art and architecture."

"And now could you pull all that together into one concise definition?"

"Give me a few years to think it over."

She lives on a mountain,

And pees like a bloody fountain,

And the hairs of her dinky-di-doo

Hang down to her knees.

After many such verses, some of which the audience sang too, the quartet left the stage, the combo took a short break, and a rather tipsy Black Swan commandeered the free stage to perform a Pavlova-style Dying Swan, without music, thumping the thin boards like a drum as she bouréed round and round in ever diminishing circles and finally collapsed and died with slowly flapping arms amid light applause and a single "Brava."

A Prime Number dressed as a cavalier asked an ARCIGAY young man in drag, "Is there a lot of intolerance in Naples?"

"Oh, yes. Too much. But nobody much cares if you're gay as long as you don't say you are."

"Is that so hard?"

"Well, yes, especially if you would like to live openly, to be honest."

"Any progress at all?"

"Not much. Southern Italy is very traditional. Single men live with their parents. But we will change it. It will just take time."

"I hope so. Telling Mamma that you're going for a walk every night before bed when you're fifty can't be any fun."

"But it is expected in many places."

The combo returned to the stage, a blue spotlight came on, and into its beam walked a silver-lamé draped, hooded-eye, blonde grand dame with a wry smile and a white fur stole that she slipped off, held up, and said into the mike, "Yes, I've still got it," before tossing it to the MC, cocking a bent leg into the slit of her gown, smiling more broadly, throwing her head back, putting the mike to her lips, and singing just three words:

Pardon me, boys …

"Marlene," several Prime Numbers shouted in unison.

She paused, shrugged her shoulders, slowly looked at the crowd, and said, "What? Something?"

They cheered and she continued.

Is that the Chattanooga Choo Choo?

"There," said John, "You see. That's glamour. One hundred percent artifice, contrivance, almost like playing children's dress-up. Jim is an ugly, pig-eyed man, but his Marlene is quite good, quite glamourous. A fantasy. Glamour is a concept, not a reality. Occasionally someone fulfills the concept briefly, but it is like an unstable element. It disappears, self-destructs, is gone, leaving only the idea."

"Yes, but fun, huh? Maybe the Sibyl of Cumae was glamourous when young. And as for Jim, yes, he's well known for his Marlene, but I can't believe that he would lug that dress and fur stole all the way here from California."

"Maybe he sent them ahead."

Marlene took a last bow, retrieved her stole, and rejoined the audience.

"George," asked Harry, "what happened to Ahmadou?"

"Oh, didn't you see? When he came off stage, several of our guys rushed him straight to that shadowy copse over there. A steady stream of fellows has been coming and going but slowing down a lot now. I heard his brothers are there too. And quite a bunch of the ARCIGAYs. I couldn't even see Ahmadou when I went over to look. He must have been in the center somewhere."

"That explains why things thinned out here for a while. Well, more power to them. Reminds me of a gay baseball game I saw once at the Russian River. Someone hit a ball into the bushes, and both teams rushed in to find it, and just never came out."

"My friend Harry, the dedicated sports fan. Say, is my mantilla dragging again?"

"Carmen, sweetheart, it is perfect."

The MC took the stage again and announced the first group from a Naples dance club.

"And now, straight from the Berlin of Sally Bowles to Naples, the Andrews Sisters."

Three towering singers, each more than seven feet tall in their Ann Sheridan fuck-me high heels and lofty blonde pompadours, with broadly padded shoulders, Clara Bow lips, and bangle bracelets marched single file to center stage, stopped, turned in unison to the footlights, saluted the audience, and launched into their first number with panache and blinding smiles.

Down in die meadow in ein itty bitty pool
Livid drei little fische und die mutter fische zu
Schvim said die mutter fische

Schvim if du kann
Und sie schvam und sie schvam right uber der damm

A door at the top of the outside stairways to the opera house opened, and Marutus came out with two older men, one of Diaghilievian proportions. All three were dressed in tuxedos. They descended the stair, and Marutus took them to William, who was talking to Carl, and introduced the executive director of the opera house and his lover, a Camorra boss.

"And this is Carl, a geologist, who has been very helpful in explaining the geologic history of Naples."

"Ah, Carlo," said the director. "I like. Hot rocks, no?"

They all laughed loudly as the Andrews Sisters sang on.

Boop boop dittum dattum vattum choo
Boop boop dittum dattum vattum choo

William and Marutus led the director and his friend through the crowd, making introductions here and there as they went. Another fellow in a tuxedo came out of the door at the top of the steps, looked quickly over the crowd below, and hurried down to the director. They spoke rapidly in Italian. The director took Marutus and William aside, and they had a brief and excited conference at the end of which the director shrugged his shoulders, threw up his hands, and then nodded affirmatively. He mounted the steps again, turned to wave to the crowd, and disappeared with his friend and the new man through the door.

"What's going on over there?" Harry asked Carl.

"I'm not sure. They seemed to be discussing someone named Marcia Trionfale. Maybe a problem with one of the singers."

Stop, said die mutter fische, you'll get lost
But die drei little fisches didn't vant to be bossed

William went up on stage, said something quietly to the combo. which stopped playing, and then to the puzzled singers, who had cut their number. They all left the stage, and William was joined by Mark and Marutus.

"Gather round here, men," Mark said into the microphone, and the partygoers moved in close to the stage. "There is a problem of some immediacy with the opera, and we have been asked to help. Marutus will explain."

He handed Marutus the microphone.

"Our supers for this special out-of-season performance presently going on are involved in a traffic accident and cannot get here in time for their entrance. The director has invited you men to step in for them. I hope that you will agree to help us in this emergency. I think William should speak now."

William took the microphone and said, "I already accepted for us. Destiny calls. We all will go on stage tonight as performers at the great San Carlo Opera dressed as we are with a little very fast extra preparation. The opera intermission is coming up, and it can be extended a little, but not much. Now here's what we do ..."

Marutus said something in William's ear.

"Oh, yes. Where is our black entertainer? I understand that he is still here somewhere. In the opera story, they have conquered Ethiopia, and we could use a black fellow."

The three naked Senegalese men came through the crowd and stood before the stage.

"Excellent," said Marutus. "There are three of you. We'll have to get some loincloths over those things, perhaps lavender loin cloths. Giuseppe can do that. And on stage, I want you boys to jump and twist. Can you jump? Yes, as high as you can. And get the hat and those shoes off. I want you barefoot. William, run them straight to Giuseppe right now."

William and the boys left, and a Cleopatra called up to Marutus.

"I have a bad hip, Marutus. You will have to excuse me."

"Ah, Cleopatra can't walk. We will get her a sedan chair. Oh, there are four Cleopatras. We will get four sedan chairs. Now we need volunteer bearers, buffed bearers, buffed bear bearers. Take off your shirts. You're eunuchs now transporting the harem."

Marutus came down from the stage and led the chattering crowd back through the basement door and into the wardrobe, where Giuseppe and three assistants made very superficial costume and makeup adjustments before moving them one at a time out into the hall where they waited excitedly. At last, all had been rushed through and were gathered together. Marutus hurried into the hall and raised his hands.

"Listen carefully. I will take you upstairs in our freight elevator to the stage wings. We will all fit in. It is an open elevator, so be careful. Stay together when you get off. I will place you in the wings behind some of our people who already are there. At my signal, you will go across the stage with them at their pace to the wings on the other side. The audience will be on your left, your captors on your right. You are trophy slaves now. Your future depends on the acceptance by your captors of your talents and charms. While on stage, I want you to express that in any way you wish. Giuseppe, what is the word that American dancers use? Swan, that's it. From Swan Lake. From drunk Englishmen spouting Shakespeare, the Swan of Avon. Vamp is another word. Chew the scenery is good too. But silence, absolute silence. Not a word. Now, here is the elevator, big enough for all of us and even the sedan chairs. Oh, no, William, my friend. No escape. I want you here too. Remember, silence. And we thank you all in advance. Break some legs."

Harry and George were at the rear of the moving mass. Harry asked quietly, "What are you doing?"

"I'm getting all this on my cell phone camera and sending it live to my grandson. He's visiting a new boyfriend in Scotland who likes opera."

"Maybe the opera people don't want you to do that?"

"Look around, darling. This is almost chaos. Nobody has time for police work. I'm going to get this whole thing, especially the stage part."

The operator closed the slat door to the elevator and it moved slowly up, majestically, into the increasingly red glow of the ceiling lights and the loudening boom of a live opera. Almost everyone developed goose bumps, eyes widened, and a thrill shot through the whole group. At the top, they all carefully left the elevator and followed Marutus to some singers waiting in the wings for their entrance and lined up behind them as he directed them to do in mime.

George nudged Harry, pointed, and mouthed the word, "Elephants."

Harry cupped his hand over George's ear and whispered "What did you expect? It's *Aida*."

On stage, Ramfis and the chorus sang their guts out and then the orchestra trumpeted the "Grand March" entrance and the chorus began, "Vieni, o guerriero vindice." Marutus grinned, raised his arm, and let it fall like a starter's flag. The Prime Numbers and their Italian gay brothers surged forward, launching themselves like birds onto virgin flights into the ethereal world of Grand Opera. An Andrews Sister broke the silence rule to say to her sisters, "Right uber die damm" as they stepped out from the wings onto the great stage of the Real Teatro di S. Carlo.

In the huge royal box, the opera director clutched his lover's knee with one hand, covered his own eyes with the other, and muttered a prayer. Behind him, Mary elbowed her dozing husband.

"Wake up, John. Something's happening."

All over the theater, the audience stirred and waked. *Aida* is, after all, a heavy, dull, and predictable nineteenth-century ham-and-eggs antique with an unrequited love theme, written by a reluctant Verdi as a commission for the Khedive of Egypt for his newish opera house in provincial Cairo. The soloists usually are physically absurd in the roles. Neapolitans, however, are famous for madly idolizing the oddest icons in the arts, sports, and politics, and there were enough Neapolitans in the audience tonight to trigger this reaction. The house watched with noisy delight as a madly dressed throng of captives entered, made obeisance to the king, and outrageously mugged the audience itself. The moving horde seemed unending, pouring from the wings, crossing the stage, and disappearing.

The front row of the orchestra seats was the first to stand, prompted by the three Andrews Sisters, each holding hands with a semi-nude black man and blowing kisses madly at individuals in that row. Soon, people were standing everywhere, applauding and cheering the marchers, who applauded them back, Russian style.

John leaned close to Mary and said, "This is what I want for 'Scream.' A real boogaloo."

Carl, in his pageboy costume, was among the first to reach the opposite wings. There he was met by Judith, dressed in a hoop skirt and Scarlet O'Hara picture hat, who took his hand.

"This way, Carl," she said loudly, there no longer being any need of stage silence because of the noisy audience.

"But, Judith," he asked, "where are we going?"

"Behind the sets, back to the other side, so that we can go around again. It will look like one long march to the audience. Come."

Carl glanced at William, who was nearby but didn't see him, and then just motioned everyone to follow him and they did. The elephants were led away, the Cleopatras—one lame but still game—climbed from their sedan chairs, followed Judith, and they all were just in time to rejoin the last of the marchers about to make their first entrance. The Grand March now was moving in almost an oval, a little Circus Maximus, a wild gay triumph.

The conductor repeated the passage again and yet again. The singers on stage looked more amused than annoyed and some came out of character. Aida looked at her watch.

At last, a laughing Marutus appeared backstage and stopped the progress, breaking the continuity so that the Grand March ended with Marie Antoinette hugging the curtain, kicking up one heel, and disappearing. Aida threw herself into the arms of Amonasro, and Radames took a deep breath in preparation for the aria in which he intercedes for the captives. The conductor raised his baton.

At that moment, the stage went black. Radames exhaled and the conductor lowered his baton. A loud drumroll was heard, three spotlights formed concentric circles center stage, focused on an amorphous, sparkling mass. An unseen soprano began a strange, vaguely oriental, lilting song, causing Carl to open his eyes widely in sudden recognition.

The glittering body lying on the stage raised an arm. Was there ever any arm so sinuous as this one as it writhed in time with the song? The audience became completely silent. The arm reached upward, and the body followed and stood, an immensely fat odalisque completely covered in a sequined harem costume, eyes heavily lined with kohl, a golden and bejeweled turban on her head. She writhed, she hooched, she hunched, she bumped and ground, she shook her great ass, she did backbends, she mimed burning her hands over imaginary candles, she raised her head and opened her big eyes, looking upward so that the whites flashed in the spots, and then she turned full front toward the royal box and began slow movements of an incredibly libidinous and prurient essence.

The San Carlo Opera executive director blushed. Not a sound from the audience marred the strange song.

Then the song slowed, faded, and ended as the odalisque collapsed in time to it onto the floor again, a final snaking arm dropping into her shapeless form, still except for rapid breathing, which caused the sequins to quiver and glitter. The spotlights snapped off, leaving the stage in blackness once more. When the regular stage lights went on again, the odalisque was gone.

There was a telling silence in the theater of the kind that happens only on the very rare occasions when an audience has been stunned by a performance. A pause. Then all hell broke loose as they screamed, applauded, shouted ten thousand bravas, and waited for the odalisque to take a curtain call.

She did not. She was never seen or heard from again. That night, the opera plodded to the end and the audience left.

Next day, Naples had another goddess to place in its unique pantheon. All over the city, they talked of the odalisque. And know what? Everyone knew that she was a man. Except for his sister and three opera electricians, only the opera director and Carl knew who he was. And they never told.

The following piece appeared in the *International Herald Tribune* next morning:

OPERA WAR HORSE UPDATED
Not Since the Castrati
By Ian Smith, Edinburgh News

NAPLES—Thursday, the Teatro di San Carlo staged the annual fund-raising performance for its foundation, unusually held in August this year to take advantage of foreign visitors. The work was an innovative production of *Aida* highlighted by an extended Grand March more elaborate than earlier versions. It featured the usual elephants but also troupes of remarkably well-trained dancers and extras dressed in costume as an historic tribute to past stars and patrons of this venerable opera house, built in 1737 by the popular Bourbon King Charles III. Of special note were participants celebrating the once famous San Carlo castrati as well as pop and other modern performers. The audience included diplomats from the city's forty-four foreign consulates, international artists, writers, and composers, and a large contingent of the rich and famous.

The caption for an accompanying photograph read, "NEW NAPLES ICON: The Grand March odalisque, seen here from the wings, took top honors at the Teatro di San Carlo production of *Aida*."

VIII. OVER THE WAVES

Carl greatly anticipated today's leg of the trip, their destination being not only a tall, conical volcanic island but an almost continuously active crater, erupting very frequent sprays of incandescent lava from an off-center position, which then tumbles down a long slide area, some of it falling even into the sea nearly three thousand feet below, where it lies hissing in the low waves, amid clouds of steam and an awful stench. This especially is spectacular at night from boats. The Prime Numbers movie group also looked forward to it because there would be screenings for them there of two old movies, one with the same name as the island.

It was 8:30 at the Naples Beverello pier where their ferry waited with gangplank extending from the midship port door to the pier. Mark was giving the captain the tickets while the Prime Numbers gathered nearby with their luggage, saying good-byes to the ARCIGAY men and other friends who had helped them transport it from the hotel to the bus to the pier. There was an exchange of presents, many kisses on both cheeks, and even a few on the lips, suggesting more than casual relationships. Invitations to California were many. Ahmadou was holding hands with George, and Giuseppe Salvatore handed Harry an envelope. The Andrews Sisters came in costume, having made the round of night clubs and not having been back to their home to change yet.

The Prime Numbers would not return to Naples on this trip but go on from the island to idyllic Taormina on Sicily and afterward begin the long flight home from Sicily too.

At last they boarded, and chose seats among the rows of them inside the huge main cabin. The gangplank was hauled aboard, the mooring lines thrown off, and the visitors on the pier waved. The boat maneuvered out through the long, narrow, breakwater-bordered channel, past the twin lighthouses at the entrance, increased speed, lifted on its hydrofoils, moving literally over the waves, across the Bay of Naples, through the strait separating Capri from the mainland Point Campanella, entered the Gulf of Salerno, and then the Tyrrhenian Sea. The course was set for Stromboli, a 130-nautical mile run from Naples that takes about four hours to complete.

After settling their luggage near their seats, Henry and Bob went to the snack bar near the stern for coffee. As they stood waiting for an attendant to show up, Bob asked Henry a question.

"A personal question, Henry, please, about your cochlear implant. Would you tell me what it's like to have a hole drilled in your skull and a computer inserted?"

Henry raised and lowered his eyebrows and, with a sigh, replied, "Oh, of course, I was out during the operation, but I was determined to make the whole procedure an interesting experience, so I overrode my anxiety with curiosity and watched everything I could just before the procedure, hoping for something interesting to happen.

"I thought of Proust in his last days. It sometimes is said that he saw death waiting for him in the corner of his room every day, as reported by his servant Celeste Albaret in a book she wrote afterward. But I have read that book, and she didn't say anything of the kind. He merely asked her once not to turn off the light because there was a horrible fat woman in the room and he wanted to be able to see.

"So, as I lay on the gurney, I wondered if Proust's horrible person might be in the prep room with me, and I looked all around for her while I was waiting for the anesthesia injection in a vein on the back of my hand. There was quite a wait. I raised my head and looked several times; nothing. There were many busy people moving around, all masked and in scrub hats so that only their eyes were exposed in the intervening slits. Suddenly, in through the hall door walked a figure much taller than the others, with broad shoulders, and with little whisps of blonde hair showing around his cap. A mask covered his lower face too. Suddenly, he looked at me with a direct gaze and our eyes locked a long moment as only gay strangers lock eyes. His eyes were the most incredible blue. Then he looked away and walked out of the room. I thought it was not my time to die after all, and it wasn't.

"But that's how I want my death to look when he comes for me—tall and blonde and blue-eyed. I would have gone with him in a heartbeat. Then a small, dark, Latina nurse gave me the injection, and it was all done when I woke later."

Frank and Bob had despaired of finding a plastic window clear enough so that they could watch the sea. At last, one of the crew opened the top half of a door midships to check something outside on the deck, and they convinced him to leave it open. They stood, talking, with forearms braced on the top of the lower half, watching the waves speed by and enjoying the wind carried into the cabin.

"So, you have a gay nephew?" Frank asked.

"Yes, and proud of it. I worked on my brother and his wife to get them to accept his homosexuality."

"Did they?"

"Yes, they were superb. He's now a fine pediatrician, living in Palm Springs with his husband, an artist. They have two sons. I see them often."

"Adopted, of course."

"Not at all. The boys are twin half-brothers, now four years old, both from eggs of the same mother, one egg fertilized by my nephew and the other by his husband. Both eggs were implanted the same day, each in a separate surrogate mother, neither one of whom was the donor."

"Superb! No fraternal competition in the womb."

"Correct. And no lack of nutrients while developing."

"Somebody did it right. Must have been very expensive."

"Actually, not as much as you might expect. Anyway, that part was entirely my contribution. The whole operation was a big family project, every step of the way, from selection of the egg donor to births."

"Do they have the same birthdays?"

"That was a slight problem because they were born two weeks apart. They get to celebrate two birthdays in the same month."

"Do they ever see the mothers?"

"Oh, yes. They are friends of the family now. We're quite open with the boys about everything."

"Two mommies and two daddies. Happy boys, I should think."

"They're spoiled rotten, but that will pass. The older one is named Rock, the younger one Star. My nephew did that. He called me a rock star in a thank you letter when he was in school."

"Every gay youth should have such a rock star in the family."

And in the first row of the passenger seats, Carl was reaching into his carry-on bag for a book when someone tapped him on the shoulder.

"Carl, can I ask you a question?"

"Oh, hello, Hal. Yeah, of course. What?"

"It's about progress and society."

"Hal, you must be the guy who is asking around with the meaning-of-life questions. Yeah?"

"Well, probably. I do want to know what other people think about some things, and asking them seems to me to be the best way to find out."

"How about a priest? That's their job."

"No, no. I've done that. They either want to get into your pants or your bank account, or they're practicing for some future sermon. They never tell you what they themselves think. If they did, they'd have a crisis of faith problem that would get them sent away to a retreat for counseling. I want something more."

"What?"

"Well, you're a scientist, a geologist, a paleontologist. You know the history of life on earth as found out by observing fossils in the rock layers that date back nearly to the beginning."

"I had some historical geology courses, and I now teach one. I know the standard information."

"Yes, but you must know how life appeared and changed into all of it we see now. The animals and plants muddling around over vast stretches of time, genes and chromosomes adapting to changing climates and conditions, anything to keep up and keep going, right? If they didn't, they died out."

"That's a little crude but not inaccurate. You seem already to have a grasp of your subject. What's the question?"

"Well, on this trip we have looked at ruins and artifacts and such made by people over the last few thousand years. And we've heard a little of what they wrote down. I see some progress, maybe even straight-line progress in the artifacts. But where's the evolution in man in this time period? Seems like all the same people to me, like us. Mark asked if we could talk to people in old Pompeii and be friends. Looked to me like we could. Almost two thousand years ago. Where's the change? Where's the evolution? What do you, yourself think about that?"

"Okay, Hal, look. Yes, once I understood some principles of genetics and something about human evolution from ape men to us. I thought that things with humans were getting better all the time and that it was evolution. But now I do not think that. I am more pessimistic. All around me, I see barbarism, in the same basic forms as it existed in the Pompeiian world but on scales that would be inconceivable to them because the human population is so enormous now by comparison to theirs. Nero, for example, that truly insane Roman emperor, never even dreamed of having the powers to destroy people in the numbers that our present-day leaders take for granted. And they seem actually to do it without hesitation. Very discouraging to me."

"But the advances?"

"All technological, not genetic. As we saw from that museum exhibit, computers existed even in the first century B.C. It's just that the Industrial Revolution has done more with them, not that humans have advanced and become more capable of making them. That's not real progress; that's simply change. Monsters still are leaders of entire countries from time to time, starting fool wars, trying to kill off entire people—but you know all that."

"Got it, Mark. So far, nobody in our group is very encouraging about humanity. Very interesting."

"Look, Hal. It is quite probable that mankind is just another species running its meaningless course on this planet. Unusually sentient perhaps, but still essentially hopeless. Perhaps biology can eventually give us another great step forward. I don't know. Perhaps humans will all just die out in the ordinary way."

"Thanks, Mark. Very helpful. I'll see you. Want to get back to my seat."

As Hal left, Greg, the actor who had read the Pliny the Younger letters to the Prime Numbers on Point Misenum, approached Mark.

"Hello, Mark. You're having a busy day. Got a moment for me?"

"Sure, Greg. Sit down here."

"Mark, one of the fellows told me that you were born in Naples. Is that correct?"

"Not quite. I was born outside the city in a provincial farm town."

"And your parents moved to America?"

"Yes, something like that. I was still a boy, but I never will forget being here."

"Mark, what is it that makes you repeatedly ask us if we think that we could understand the old Romans if we had the chance to meet them?"

"My family was in the Naples area for centuries, but we don't know if they were there far back enough for them to have been Roman. If it was, I likely have their genes and would fit into Roman society that way myself. However, we may be too different by now from them. I don't know, but I would like to know. It is, however, more or less a casual interest, a subject that I thought might tie this tour together a little. I have gotten quite a lot of input from our group."

"Got it. You know, Mark, there is something different culturally about Roman society that makes me think we might not fit in so well. Something other than the fact that they were such a warrior-based people."

"Good. You're the first one who has said that. Everyone else just assumes that we still are the same people. Please go on."

"I think that we now live in a secular society, by and large, despite some argument I would get about that statement. The Romans, however, seem to have considered that their everyday world and the mythical world of their gods and goddesses were so close that there might be everyday contact with the gods themselves. And then, after Julius Caesar, when the Empire got started under Augustus, it was not so uncommon for people to believe that some of them actually became gods, at least after death, real gods, not just something honorific. Temples were set up for them and they were worshiped, some even before they died. I have read that generals in their famous triumphs in Rome had a slave stand behind them in the same chariot who kept repeating 'Remember, you are a man.' This was to keep them from suddenly feeling that they had become gods. Hadrian had temples built for his dead lover where he was worshiped as a god, apparently quite seriously. Cleopatra was the Living Isis, an actual goddess, while she lived. Alexander became an Egyptian god when he was in his early twenties. Nero thought that he had become a god while he was still alive. Perhaps there is some skepticism left behind by the contemporary writers, but apparently it was taken very seriously by the populace. Isn't that so entirely, so basically different from the way we think today that we, ourselves, would not understand those old Romans, much less be able to associate comfortably with them?"

Mark nodded enthusiastically and shook Greg's hand.

"Ah, Greg, very good. Excellent. Of course, that is exactly what I'm talking about when I ask these questions. At first thinking, such differences seem minor, cultural, and superficial, but you are quite correct to question if that is true. There might be a genetic basis that would differ from ours so radically that we would seem like aliens to them. I suspect that there is a religion gene because of the extremes of belief—some people have it, some don't. Maybe the Romans had too much of it for compatibility with us. My thoughts are pretty close to yours. Perhaps we are so fundamentally different from the people of ancient Rome that we would not fit into that society at all. However, I'm not sure. Just think of their official use of augurs."

Mark and Greg continued talking as the ferry skimmed on toward Stromboli.

"Mark, who is your favorite writer?"

"Constantine Cavafy, hands down, with James Joyce a close second."

Above the passenger's cabin, in the captain's private office on the bridge, Judith and her brother shifted in their leather reclining chairs and continued gossiping over coffee with the first mate as the elegantly shaped ferry skimmed along on its course. Inside the main cabin, the Prime Numbers gathered in groups to talk, looked out the cloudy plastic windows at the passing coast, read, slept, and walked about, almost indistinguishable from the other passengers. Then, with a slight change of course, the ferry veered toward the open sea, Campania disappeared behind them, and the ship became the center of a giant blue Tyrrhenian Sea bowl under a dome of similarly hued blue, blue sky.

* * *

John was walking back and forth on the patio of their Naples cottage, talking on his cell phone, a conference call to his associates in New York. Mary, sitting nearby, listened carefully. The reception was better outside the house, but even there calls sometimes were dropped.

"But we can screen them somehow at the stage door to make sure there are no guns or bombs. And we could advertise and assign them nights. Any amateur or professional who wanted to do it would be considered … I *do* think it would work. It was smashing here last night for *Aida*. A sensation. One of the most astonishing performances I have ever seen anywhere. Just amazing … Well, I couldn't find the artistic director today, but I did talk with the opera house director. He said that they all were volunteers, a wholly unrehearsed performance … Yes, he is out of town for a few days, and I will see him when he gets back. And pump him for details. I can tell you that this is what we need: a real boogaloo inserted into the performance—a slot in the musical, one that will be different every night or few nights, an entirely new idea for Broadway musicals. Think of the publicity. Something that would recapture the impromptu feeling of the original boogaloos. It would be sensational … Yes, living theater, improvisation of a sort but specifically for our show. We would have overall control … Indeed, I do think it would work for an out-of-town opening … Yes, great progress with the rest of the musical. It is coming together. I will have it for you on schedule … Thank you, gentlemen … And you too."

"Well?" asked Mary, as John clicked off.

"I think they bought it. Cautious but intrigued. They will contact the American ambassador here for his opinion about the *Aida*, but I'd say we're on."

* * *

As the hydrofoil reached the halfway mark on its run to Stromboli, Mark was considering a nap when one of his group approached him.

"Listen, Mark, I want to thank you for last night. No one has talked of anything else. I don't know how William did it. I looked for him all over the boat to thank him but can't find him. Isn't he with us?"

"No. I'm not sure how much he wants you to know, but he is away at a place near Naples for a few days with Marutus. I think that they may be thinking of becoming serious about one another. I thought everyone knew. Anyway, we won't see him again until the flight home, but you can thank him then."

"Good for him. Both he and Marutus are numbers. And I heard from someone back home that Marutus gets around and is supposedly—umm—big. Very big."

"Yes, well, I don't know about that, but I do wish them well. My problem now is how to handle this picture problem."

"What picture problem?"

"The one of the fat dancer last night that was in the Herald Trib this morning. Somebody on the opera house staff told the wire service boys that one of our guys took it, and the calls to me were burning up the hotel lines before breakfast this morning. I just said they were mistaken and stopped answering. I suppose they will be back on the telephone when we get to our next hotel."

"Oh, is that all? George took that picture. Why?"

"My god, it was George? George was taking pictures? How?"

"With his cell phone camera. He sent them live to his gay grandson in Scotland who likes opera."

"Them? More than one?"

"Oh, yeah. He got the whole thing from the moment we got on the elevator until the fat lady's dance ended. A bunch of us looked at some of it in the hotel last night. Very funny."

"Get George over here right now. He'll be richer than Croesus if he handles this properly."

* * *

Marutus slowed and pulled the little car into the parking space of an overlook, turned to William, and said, "Let's get out." They both did, Marutus unfolding his long legs with some difficulty as usual. The car top was up because of the occasional rainfall that morning, and their leather bags strapped to the luggage rack had blue plastic sheeting neatly covering them for protection. It was William's first trip along the dramatic Amalfi coastal road.

The day had started lazily for them, luxuriously slowly after the madness of the night before at the opera. Patrick had brought them coffee in bed and had packed the two small cases for their trip, asking about a few things for William. He knew from long experience exactly what Marutus would wish to take. The three of them had gone up in the elevator, Patrick carrying the two bags and William an orange that he impulsively had taken from a bowl on the way out of the apartment. The doorman had brought the car, and he and Patrick had wrapped and put the suitcases on the rack. Marutus had gotten behind the wheel and William beside him in the passenger seat, and they had driven out of Naples, through Sorrento, over the crest of the peninsula, and dropped down to the road that clings to the outer coast.

"Those little islands," said Marutus as they stood together, shoulders touching, at the overlook, "are called Li Galli, perhaps meaning the roosters, as the locals say, but more likely something else lost in history such as the eunuch priests of the powerful mother goddess Cybele, also called galli. Odysseus supposedly passed them and their then-resident singing sirens while tied to his ship's mast—wanna try that sometime, babe?—and they have a long history with gay men. In the last century, first Massine and then Nureyev lived there, Rudi going occasionally down the coast to see Vidal at his aerie in Ravello, the town we are going to now. I will point out the Vidal place to you when we get there. Shall we?"

They got back in the car, Marutus started the engine, pulled out into traffic, and they were off once again. William took the orange from the car pocket, peeled it, held a section before Marutus, and put it into his opened mouth. They both laughed as Marutus chewed and swallowed it.

"Really?" asked William over the engine noise. "Rope?"

Out to sea, a tiny speck trailing a white wake was the hydrofoil bound for Stromboli with the Prime Numbers aboard.

* * *

"Mark, have you seen those signs on the beach road?"

The Prime Numbers had arrived on Stromboli, checked into the seaside La Sirenetta Hotel, and were having an early dinner at separate tables in the hotel restaurant. Harry and George had gone walking on the beach across the street from the hotel and were a little late coming to dinner.

"Which signs, George?"

"The signs telling you to go uphill when the tsunami siren sounds?"

Mark smiled. "Yes, of course I have seen them. Look, why don't you and Harry bring chairs from that table and sit with us? There is room at our table."

They did that, and Mark continued. "There are tsunamis here every few years, caused by a submarine landslide on that great slope of broken pieces of loose lava below the crater we saw when we were coming in on the ferry."

"Well, what happens? Anything like the recent Indian Ocean tsunamis? Are they dangerous?"

"Everyone at the beach level goes uphill to a waiting area. When the danger is over, the siren sounds an all clear and everyone comes down again. Simple."

"This whole restaurant is almost on the beach. What happens here?"

"I was told that last time the waves took all the old tables and chairs out to sea and the hotel replaced them with these spiffy new ones. Aren't they great?"

"Uh, Mark, Stromboli is strange."

"Yes, so it has been said. We will hear all about the volcano tomorrow at ten AM when Carl takes us to the volcano museum just down the street. There are some American volcanologists there who will talk to us about their research on Stromboli. Meanwhile, enjoy tonight's glow from the crater. There is a minor eruption almost hourly, throwing up sprays of molten lava."

"And if we hear a siren in the night?"

"Please, wait and ask me that question at breakfast."

* * *

Someone had once asked Frederick what it was like being gay in a straight world, being in the closet.

"I hated it. Every moment, every hour, every day, every year. I hated it."

In rural New England, young Frederick hadn't known yet why he seemed to be different. His father knew that he was discontent, but not why either, and advised him about it.

"Son, just put on the old ball and chain. Marry. Everybody does. Things have a way of sorting themselves out then. You'll see."

So Frederick, certainly not the brightest person, had married. Soon the first child came and then the second, both sons. He brought home the bacon, his wife took it away from him to run the household, run his life. She worked with her mother to make his existence a living hell, a cliché. Year after year after year this went on.

The first time Frederick came to Palm Springs on a special assignment was an epiphany. To him, it seemed to be paradise, almost a whole town of gay men. He got through the ten-day job, and when it was time to leave, he told his new friends how he felt.

"Well, here I go back into the straight world. I hate it."

So they gave him some gay straight talk, based on their own experiences and those of friends. The sons were just out of college, had their first jobs, and were independent. The wife was having an affair with their married minister. Frederick went home, made a few quiet arrangements, and left his wife a brief note on the cracked Formica dining table, part of a set his mother-in-law had given them for a wedding present.

"Here's a bankbook for an account in your name with enough money in it to last you a year. I have paid down the mortgage on the house and removed my name from the title. You will get some divorce papers to sign soon. If you do not sign them, I do not care. I have gone away forever to start a new life. Yours truly, Frederick R. Smith."

Once in Palm Springs again, he had accepted a job with a decorating firm, something he was good at and liked, and rented the guest house of a gay married couple, both men. They took him to a Prime Numbers meeting, he had joined, and when much later the trip to Naples was floated, he had signed on, a happy camper, a liberated man, his jockstrap burned, New England behind him forever.

And as he sat through the melodramatic old film titled *Stromboli* being shown in a darkened room off the lobby of the La Sirenetta Hotel on *Stromboli* itself, being shown for the benefit of the Prime Numbers' movie group, the Kay Francis Society, he knew from long experience what Ingrid Bergman meant when she said three lines in her heavy Swedish accent.

"These are not my people. I do not know why I am here. I want to go away, far away."

And Frederick smiled quietly to himself.

* * *

If one concedes that the four cardinal directions, all human artifacts, can be applied to a conical natural feature, then Vesuvius can be said to have such sides. It's as simple as squaring the circle, an early Greek mathematical accomplishment. The seaward side is on the south and southwest and in Roman times had the towns of Pompeii and Herculaneum. Patrician and royal Roman villas also were here because of the views, the ocean breezes, and ease of access by sea. More recently, this side too had royal palaces built by Naples royalty and their contemporaries in the then-still country to get away from city life.

The opposite side of Vesuvius, generally called the north side, faces the great agricultural plain of Campania and is a less-desirable living location because the sea is absent and the climate therefore is more extreme and the views less lovely. It also could be called the dark side of Vesuvius because of the prevalence of organized crime in the area. Yet here too, there are many villages, some of them rivaling their contemporary seaside neighbors in picturesque charm.

Of course, none of Vesuvius should be populated at all because of the volcanic dangers, but since the last eruptive cycle ended in the mid-twentieth century and memories are short and land cheap in such dangerous areas, people do live there. The government regularly warns them of the difficulty of evacuation when the next eruption occurs because of inadequate roads.

It was to the dark side of Vesuvius that Frank Bones took Red for dinner. They drove into the village of Somma Vesuviana through the milling *passeggiata* crowds, found a parking place on a steep street, and walked back downhill to a restaurant named Arlecchino where Bones knew the owner. They were shown by him through the main dining area and onto a back patio with tables overhung by an arbor with fruiting kiwi vines, an import dating from a time when many Italians worked in Australia. A lighted candle in a glass bowl was on their table.

Here, they were the only diners, it still being twilight and early for dinner by local custom. Bones ordered the specialty of the house—fried pizza—and a fine local wine, Catalanesca. He and the owner spoke briefly of a nearby property on which Bones had been collecting plants buried by the 79 A.D. eruption. Then, the owner left and they were alone.

What does a determined lover say to his intended, who is just as firm that they will never be lovers, and each already knows the other's position from long association? Very little at this meeting. Each had suffered physical wounds at the hands of the other, and there was some curiosity about these.

"Did you get protheses?" asked Red first.

"Yes, big ones, quite satisfactory. And I have regular testosterone injections," was the reply. "And you, did the circumcision heal properly?"

"Not at first. Some of your stitches pulled out, and there was a mild infection. Now it is okay."

An odd conversation, but brutally honest and without rancor. The food and wine arrived and were eaten. The men talked of other things.

"When will you be finished in Naples?"

"At the earliest, this time next year."

"Will you see me when you return to San Francisco?"

"It is unlikely that I will either return or see you."

"I am here for three more weeks. Can we meet again?"

"Yes, at least twice more."

Questions and answers, brief and pertinent, informative, almost catechismal. Then dinner was over, and the host was paid and thanked. Bones drove them back to the city, took Red to his hotel, and returned to his own condo.

Before they parted for the night, there was a repeat promise of further meetings.

* * *

The old canard, "Bad roads, good people; good roads, bad people," suggests that people who make it over bad roads may have a strength of character and a perseverance that people who drive only on good roads do not. This broadly might be applied to marine destinations. Out-of-the-way ports may have interesting residents, institutions, and visitors lacking in more accessible ports. On Stromboli, just such a place is Barbablu, a two-story inn near the upper village piazza with six somewhat North African style rooms for rent upstairs and downstairs a tiny bar and larger restaurant, the latter extending outside under a grape arbor in good weather. World-class characters run the place, and world-class characters patronize it. It later reminded a Kay Francis Society member of the old film *Beat the Devil*.

"The whole cast belongs here," he commented.

The tenor of Barbablu is tolerance and excellence, set by the owners and staff. An outstanding cuisine and wines, both a mixture of Campanian and Veneto origins, excellent conversation, superb service, and the promise of comradeship is all tucked away on an island happily bypassed by Mr. and Mrs. America-on-Tour. Who could ask for anything more?

Carl had been uninterested in seeing the Stromboli film, a movie made before he was born, so he skipped the after-dinner showing at the La Sirenetta Hotel and went exploring by himself. He followed the beach road back to the pier and took the road leading uphill from there, which he had noticed when the ferry docked. First he passed numerous open roadside shops that provided ample light to see the way. Then he came to a large and level piazza with a church on one side. Next, he followed the road leading away from it and around the hillside. A fetching-looking barefoot number in what Carl imagined might be white Tunisian pajamas with tassels was coming from the other direction, and their eyes locked for a moment before the young man turned into a building and Carl followed. It was Barbablu.

He got a drink at the bar and for a while talked to the louche young man, someone with an education who appeared to have gone native. Then, as his eyes grew accustomed to the dimness of the room, he noticed his Naples friend, the fat man, sitting alone on a bench running along one wall, apparently lost in thought while nursing a glass of wine.

Carl excused himself and approached the fat man, who looked up with a smile.

"Carl," he said, "how nice to meet you here. Please sit down."

"Sir," Carl began, after sitting, "you are full of surprises. I didn't expect to see you again."

"But I expected to see you, and here we are."

"Yes," continued Carl. "Very nice, indeed. I want to tell you how superb I thought you were at the opera. Quite magnificent. How did you do that?"

The fat man merely smiled but obviously was pleased.

"I mean, how did you arrange the blackout and the spots and the music? I assume that your sister was the singer, but what about the drums? Where did you learn to dance like that?"

"One has friends everywhere," the fat man replied. "How do you like this establishment?"

They talked casually for a few more minutes about Barbablu and its history, and then the fat man asked a direct question.

"Carl, how would you like to see my little room upstairs?"

Although the encounter never progressed quite to a love affair, the ensuing intimacy deepened their friendship, just as had been planned, all of which later became obvious to Carl as events unfolded.

Sometime after midnight, Carl walked through a pouring rain from Barbablu back to his own hotel, showered, and went to bed.

* * *

Little Ethel, happy at last? She had married Hank at the Palermo stop, sister Jane in attendance, studiously weeping. It had all seemed so thrilling, so beautiful, so adventurous, so right. She would tell her mother later. But the e-mail from her mother came first: "STAY AWAY FROM THAT MAN. CHIEF SMITH HERE SAYS HE WAS MARRIED FIVE TIMES IN THE LAST SIX YEARS AND WIDOWED FIVE TIMES. WE HAVE CONTACTED INTERPOL. CALL ME AT ONCE. MOM."

Instead of calling anyone, Ethel had demanded her passport from the ship's office, put it in her purse, and fled the docked ship, taking only the clothes she was wearing. In the city, she had found a travel agency and booked the next ferry to Stromboli, an offbeat destination, she was told. She took a taxi to the pier and boarded the ferry, which got underway within the hour. They would never find her on some obscure Sicilian island, she told herself.

Once on Stromboli, she had shown surprising initiative and asked the first driver she saw loading passengers and luggage onto a Piaggio Ape jitney for a hotel recommendation. One of the passengers overheard her and recommended her own hotel, the La Sciara, and there she went, a somewhat rundown place, hidden away in a residential area. After registering ("My bags will come later") and being shown to her room, she had lain down, exhausted, and fallen into a deep sleep.

* * *

It was 3:17 AM. Two sharp jolts shook Stromboli, causing chandeliers to sway and a few objects to fall from shelves. At the La Sirenetta Hotel, there were shouts, lights went on, doors opened to outside hallways, and the alarmed Prime Numbers in their upper floor rooms poured out dressed in sleeping gear, towels, and hotel robes. Mark and Carl ran past them, through the hall, and down the series of steps and intervening patios to the hotel desk on the street floor.

"Woo-woo and wow, Barney Google and tomato aspic. An earthquake. Darlings, we might as well have stayed in Palm Springs," Harry exclaimed loudly as he came out of his room, banging the door behind him against the wall.

A few seconds later, Mark and Carl hurriedly returned.

"The manager says it is okay," Mark announced, walking down the hall, repeating himself to each group. "Happens all the time. Nothing to worry about unless we hear a siren. Go back to bed. We'll talk about it at breakfast."

Carl trailed him a little, asking several groups, "A four point three on the Richter scale, don't you guess?" and adding to Harry and George, "Nice, huh? I love earthquakes."

"You love earthquakes," squealed George. "Why? They scare the shit out of us."

"But," responded Carl, "if you can learn to control your initial panic, you can observe whatever has happened. Were there ground noises, what damage, could you stand, and so forth? Think of them as being like orgasms, something to be slowed down and enjoyed and savored. Don't lose your head like kids do. Play the Zen exercise called stop-the-world."

"Carl," commented Harry as he and George turned to go back into their room, "you're something else."

Peace and quiet soon returned to the hotel, and the only sound once again was the rhythmic susurrus of the low waves as they advanced and retreated, noisily grinding the black scoriaceous lava pebbles of the beach. The sky above the crater glowed a little brighter, and a slight sulphurous odor moved down the slope and into the community. Somewhere a raven cawed, dreaming of a meal of stranded, rotting fish.

IX. LIGHTHOUSE OF THE MEDITERRANEAN

A small flock of ravens had arrived in the spring, the first that anyone except Stromboli's very oldest residents could remember seeing there. They came in at dawn, black dots against the rising sun at first, then a little larger, like black stars forming constellations that changed shape slowly and constantly. Two fishermen in a skiff watched as they passed overhead. The big black birds landed on the black volcanic sand and immediately began noisily strutting about looking for edible flotsam along the strand and abandoned picnic scraps on the beach beyond. They soon became accepted as just another species of bird on Stromboli, and as the summer progressed, their numbers nearly doubled. One of the village boys said he had seen them carrying sticks for nests in the abandoned vineyard terraces high above the village. Another said that they roosted in the lava cliffs higher up. Everyone got used to them and their raucous calls except the beach dogs, which joyfully charged them as interlopers whenever they heard or saw them. The ravens quickly learned that if they were quiet and didn't move, they were invisible to the dogs, black birds against black sand. And then in late summer, one evening they … but that is getting too far ahead of the story. Let's go back a little.

* * *

"Hi, Frederick," said Harry as he and George walked down the hall after breakfast, dressed in shorts and sandals, towels around their necks, "We're going to the nude beach. Wanna come?"

"Do I! Wait a minute while I get my bathing suit."

* * *

Fewer Prime Numbers showed up at the little volcano museum than Carl had expected, but he did understand that they had interests other than geology. Still, he had a substantial group since some other guests in the hotel had asked to tag along, and he had welcomed them.

The museum was in an old house on the beach road between the hotel and the pier. It was small but nicely funded by the government as well as privately and seen as not only educational about the island and its volcano but also with functions in civil protection and the local economy since evacuation procedures were explained here and the guides required for an ascent to the crater had a desk where they could be hired.

At the moment, Carl had his group gathered around some wall photos and diagrams of the little offshore island everyone had admired from the hotel.

"This is a photograph of Strombolicchio, the volcanic neck that sits in the sea about one kilometer off the hotel beach. The next figure is a cut-away diagram showing that it once was the central core of a volcano, one that had sloping sides and was quite large. Over time, the lava in the neck of the volcano cooled as it became inactive. This lava is what we see today, a natural cast of the opening through which molten lava came up. The outer slopes of the volcano were less resistant to weathering and have completely weathered away, mostly from the action of surf undercutting them so that they collapsed into the sea. The outer volcano simply disappeared, leaving only the lava stub, which is the present island. Eventually this too will be reduced by the waves to a rocky reef.

"You can hire boats on the beach to take you out to visit Strombolicchio, where I understand you can climb up ladders and stairs to the broad summit and examine the lighthouse there. I also am told that the water around the island is very clear and that it is a favorite place for snorkelers and divers because of the many kinds of sea life clinging to and swimming near the rock. Any questions?"

"So, it is a dead volcano?" someone asked.

"Yes, it is the lava core of a dead volcano, a natural cast of the conduit in which the lava rose."

Another question: "How old is it?"

"Strombolicchio is about two hundred and four thousand years old. Lava yields absolute dates because some radioactive elements that form in it decay at a known rate. At that time, Stromboli itself was not yet above sea level. By about one hundred sixty thousand years ago, Stromboli had emerged above the sea and became a twin island with Strombolicchio.

"And now, this next exhibit has a view of the active craters …"

Thus they progressed through the museum exhibits, eventually talking to the resident researchers about Stromboli and other Mediterranean volcanoes.

Someone asked a young, statuesque female researcher a question about Santorini.

"I have been to Santorini and was told there that it once was the biggest volcanic island in the Mediterranean. Is that correct?"

She replied, "Yes, the Santorini volcano was enormous. And its final eruption must have been spectacular. This occurred in about 1645 B.C. during the Late Bronze Age. About seven cubic miles of molten rock was erupted, emptying a magma chamber so large that most of the volcano collapsed into it."

"Hey," a Prime Number said, "a caldera, right? Carl has been telling us about calderas. See, Carl? I remembered caldera."

"Yes, a caldera. Enormous. This event destroyed the advanced Minoan civilization. Historians postulate that we would be speaking other languages here today if that eruption had not occurred. Changed the course of history and so forth. That explosion was followed by a little dark age, and then Greek civilization took over. Alexander the Great and all. You know the rest. And perhaps Santorini—the original volcano, that is—is the basis for the Atlantis legend."

"Could that happen to Stromboli?"

"Anything is possible here. The government has had to remove everyone from the island in the past when they felt there was danger. The consensus among scientists is that the nearly continuous little eruptions you have observed take the pressure off and prevent a great eruption. However, we really have little idea what actually is happening down below. If a major amount of lava was injected all at once, then there would be trouble."

Mark spoke up, saying, "We are going by boat just before sunset tonight to anchor offshore and hope that the crater throws out enough lava to be of interest. Can we depend on seeing something?"

"Oh, indeed, yes," she answered. "There will be explosions, glowing red lava thrown up in brilliant sprays. Stromboli isn't called Lighthouse of the Mediterranean for nothing. Perhaps some of it will tumble down the slope as far as the sea and create steam. Your boatman knows that it is illegal to anchor too close."

"I hope so," said someone in the back.

"Say," a Prime Number said, "you seem to know a lot about Santorini. Been there?"

She grinned, shook her hair, and replied, "Oh, yes. I was a summer tour guide on a ship when I was in school in Switzerland. The pay was schoolgirl allowance, you know. I once found somebody to play with, so I stopped off on Santorini for a few days."

"All right," said someone amid the laughter.

As they all were leaving the museum, one of the researchers approached Carl.

"You the geologist?" he asked.

"Yes," Carl replied.

"Any experience with harmonic tremors?"

"A little from thesis work on the Long Valley caldera in California."

"Would you take a look at our most recent seismograph records?"

"Sure. I'm through with this group for the day now."

* * *

"Like it?"

Marutus had driven them inland a few miles from the coast, top down again, up and up more winding roads, and finally into Ravello, where he had parked in a public lot, flagged down an attendant with a three-wheeled Apes, indicated the luggage rack, said "*Cimbrone*," and handed him some bills. The man had removed the bags and driven away with them. Marutus and William had put the top up on the car, locked it, and, Marutus guiding them, they had walked almost a mile up a long, cobbled pedestrian street, past houses and restaurants and shops, and through ornate iron gates into a huge, mature formal garden, and finally up the steps and into the villa near the center of the garden. Two stylish ladies had risen from behind desks and shook hands with Marutus, who had kissed each of them on both cheeks. He had introduced them to William, accepted the single iron key the ladies handed him, and given an instruction of one word.

"Tea."

Check-in was never so simple.

"Like it? I love it, babe," said William, walking about in the large living room of their suite, trailing his fingers along the backs of chairs and couches, looking through the doorway into the bedroom where their bags were already on luggage holders at the foot of each bed, and pausing at the entrance to the balcony that overlooked a verdant canyon and part of the town.

There was a knock at the door, a tea wagon was wheeled through and out onto the balcony, the attendant left, and Marutus called from the bathroom, where he was washing his face.

"I hope there are enough sandwiches, Will."

"Oh, I think so, quite enough if you hurry. None if you don't."

Marutus came outside, drying his hands on a towel, leaned over and bussed William, and sat down opposite him at the iron table.

"This should pick us up. And then I want to show you something outside."

Later, that something turned out to be a walk through part of the enormous garden to an antique, life-sized marble statue of the goddess Ceres placed in the center of the path.

"Look at what she is holding casually in her hand," said Marutus.

"Ah, wheat, I think."

"Look closer."

William bent over and peered.

"My god. And a poppy capsule. You don't think … ?"

"Carved in stone, right here now before your eyes. It must have meant something."

And then they mounted a few steps behind the statue and stood on a long terrace at the very edge of the tall cliff, more than a thousand feet above the sea, with an uninterrupted view of the blue sky, the blue sea, and a long, long line of white clouds on the distant horizon.

"Zowie!" exclaimed William in amazement at the scene.

Three late-middle-aged Italian ladies at the far end of the terrace were speaking loudly to one another.

"What are they saying?" asked William.

"Oh, she said that this must be the highest terrace in the whole world. They are thrilled to be here, happy that the estate park is open to the public this afternoon."

"Marutus," said William. "be a good fellow and walk my little digital camera down there and ask them if you could take their picture and send it to them. I don't see a camera anywhere among them."

"Ah, ha, William. Such thoughtfulness. A surprise to me, a nice surprise. Give me the camera."

And thus, two weeks later, three ladies in Pesaro received souvenir snapshots of their visit to the Terrace of Infinity on the edge of the gardens of the wonderfully luxurious Villa Cimbrone.

* * *

George, Harry, and Frederick lay propped up on their elbows, side by side in a row, facing the sea, towels beneath them to protect them from the scratchy sand.

"Well, this isn't very exciting. Just us and those girls."

"It's early yet."

"I bet it doesn't get better."

"But Taormina is next. I hear it does get better there."

"Darlings, you don't leave California in search of blow jobs."

"Speak for yourself."

"Oh, Mary, get your ass out of your head."

Frederick interrupted Harry and George by asking, "What's the film tomorrow night? I thought that the one last night was boring."

"Yes. Boring. Tomorrow will be *Vulcano*, starring a young Anna Magnani. A much better film. She plays a prostitute exiled from Naples to her home island of Vulcano, which is just over that way a few miles. Being sent to live in your hometown is an awful punishment, agreed? Not a cheerful future."

"*Stromboli*, last night's film, wasn't cheerful either."

Harry picked this up. "Well, it was miscast. Ingrid Bergman hadn't a clue what was expected of her in Italian films. Anna Magnani was cast first in it and was furious when she was dropped. And Bergman also replaced her as director Rossellini's mistress, all three of them married, with children, to other people. Prudes all over the world clucked in secret delight. In revenge, Magnani made the film *Vulcano*, a somewhat similar story on a nearby island. A tangled tale, very southern Italy."

"Yes, straights have the messiest lives, don't they? Marriage doesn't mean a thing to them."

"I'm told that Italians call it keeping life interesting," added Frederick.

"Harry, where'd you get the book? I haven't seen that, have I?"

"Not yet. I just took it from the giveaway shelf in the lobby while we were waiting for Fred. Wanna look? Here."

"*The Decline of Sodomy*? Darling, what a wonderful title but what a dreadful concept."

* * *

"But Jane, I ..."

"Don't you hesitate for this one. It still can be saved."

"But Jane, we ..."

"I have worked it out. You will take the early ferry to Stromboli tomorrow as planned and find her. You will see that she disappears, we don't care how. Into the sea or—they say there's a volcano there that people go see at night—into the volcano, it doesn't matter how. No body, no crime, no problem. I stay with the cruise and you return to it at the next port. They never will have missed you on the ship, and I will swear that you were with me all the time. You will be the heartbroken widower and heir again. Very simple. The marriage is always the hard part. We have that. Am I not right?"

"Yes, I guess so. I can do that. I will have to get my passport."

"Here, Hank, baby, I already did that. Now I have to telephone the hotels on Stromboli to find out where she is. Our purser got me a list."

* * *

Some of the private houses on the street between the church and Barbablu have facades flush with the street. The house where Roberto Rosselini and Ingrid Bergman lived is like that, with the stoop just above the street. Others are nicely set back, some of them an interesting distance, with walls at the street so that they form a private compound. The fat man and Carl stood before the tall blue gate of one of the set-back ones just three houses beyond Barbablu in the direction of the church.

"Knock again, Carl. Maybe they didn't hear us."

Carl knocked sharply again. And yet again. There was no response. Finally, the fat man lifted the latch, pushed open the gate, and together they entered and walked up a long sidewalk to the one-story house. The front door, curiously on the side of the house, was open.

"Ciao," called the fat man, putting his head inside.

No one replied, but in a moment a young woman with a basket of stiff clothing just off the line came through another door, nodded at them, and placed the basket on a table next to an ironing board in the covered outside patio.

"Yes?" she asked, wiping her hands on her apron.

"Yes," repeated the fat man, "we were told that we might be able to buy capers here."

"Ah, that would be my brother. Pat!" she called loudly.

A tall, thin figure appeared in the doorway of a shed off the patio, hesitated, and then approached them quietly. His sister spoke to him in Italian, smiled, and then returned to the house. Patroclus smiled too and motioned for them to follow him across the patio. At the door to the shed, he held up a hand for them to wait, and went inside. He quickly reappeared, carrying a medium-sized plastic container by both handles, which he put down on a nearby stool with a grunt.

"Capers," he said after removing the top and motioning for them to look.

The caper plant now ranges throughout the warmer parts of the Mediterranean, and less commonly has been planted in other parts of the world. It originated in Iraq or perhaps upper Egypt, or maybe the Russian steppes, and has been used as a cooking ingredient for several thousand years. The caper itself is the preserved flower bud. The flowers are delicate and quite lovely, although small, and have a beautiful purple tinge. In Italy, the bud is picked traditionally on the day before the flower is due to open, hence the saying "A caper flower is a caper lost." Large buds have a more robust flavor than small ones. The picked buds are placed in an open container, mixed with sea salt, and a little water is added. In a couple of weeks, one is removed, rinsed, and tasted. If the taste is not bitter, the whole lot is rinsed and then put in a mixture of brine made up of vinegar, salt, and water, where it remains indefinitely until the capers are needed for cooking. The container Patroclus brought contained capers at this finished stage.

Patroclus acquired the capers almost casually from feral plants by the road, in vacant lots, and from walls where they grew between stones while he was on the way to school, the beach, on errands for his mother, and the like. He simply pinched them off with thumbnail and forefinger and put them in his pocket. Once home again, he emptied his pockets into the container. Local restaurants, including Barbablu, bought the finished product from him, giving him an allowance-like income more than adequate for a schoolboy on Stromboli.

The fat man explained all this to Carl and bought a plastic bag of the capers.

Afterward, as they all walked down the path to leave, Carl asked what the plants were like, adding that he had never seen one. Patroclus pointed at once to a plant growing beside the walk that Carl would have mistaken for a weed. On closer inspection, there were buds and flowers and little fruits, which Carl instantly recognized as the caper berries he had first eaten in Naples. Later, Carl would see caper plants all over the Mediterranean area and beyond, in vacant lots and alongside walks and roads, but most typically cascading down the walls of churches and palaces where they took root between the ancient building stones. He would learn that they even grew between the stones of the Wailing Wall in Israel.

At the gate they said good-byes and shook hands with the young man, who closed the gate behind them as they walked into the street.

"How old is Patroclus?" asked Carl.

"About seventeen, I would say," replied the fat man, smiling slightly. "Handsome, no?"

"Yes, indeed. But did you see his eyes, his irises? The color of mother-of-pearl and almost iridescent. Very unusual. I did see him once before, yesterday from my hotel room balcony. He was goofing around on the beach across the street, playing some kind of a kissing game with boys his age, everyone laughing. It looked like he was showing them how men could kiss one another by letting him kiss them. They were curiously experimenting, but afterwards the other boys would feign nausea, with howls of laughter."

"Carl, I wanted you to see the capers today and to meet Patroclus. And, yes, I did see his eyes. Like opals. What time are you on for your dinner party tonight at Barbablu?"

In the property they had just left, a small dust devil passed through, leaving a little weather vane in the garden spinning counterclockwise.

* * *

Older houses on Stromboli still have cisterns, which once collected runoff from roofs when rain was the only water source. Some still function and serve as emergency supplies. Now there is a reservoir that holds the primary water for the larger community on the island and there no longer is the former inconvenience from periodic droughts. Still, residents and visitors are asked to limit water use. The water for the reservoir is brought in by a tanker ship that collects it on the mainland. This ship, named the *Star of Lipari* after a nearby island, is registered in Naples and has the appearance of a small freighter. It arrives regularly, anchors from the bow off the beach below the La Sirenetta Hotel, and runs a second line from the stern to a large iron ring on the seaward side of an old cement pier for stability. A large hose from the ship is brought floating through the normally calm sea and clamped onto a pipe protruding from the pier, and the water is pumped uphill to the reservoir, from which gravity feeds it downhill again to the houses below. As the water is pumped out of the ship's tanks, the waterline creeps down the lightening hull. Next day, the emptied ship leaves for the mainland to refill, and the process is repeated as often as necessary.

The captain of the *Star of Lipari* sometimes honored special delivery requests and this day had brought a small boat on deck for someone. That someone was the fat man's sister, Judith. It was Judith who now was on deck examining the boat and talking with the captain, an old friend.

"Yes, we want it pulled up on the beach near the pier and one of your men posted there to guard it for a few hours. We will come take possession of it after dark tonight and relieve him. He can help us launch it. Incidentally, when do you sail?"

"At dawn, as always."

"Very good. Do not delay this one time, please."

"We never miss a sailing."

"Excellent. Now if I just may go in the boat as you take it to the beach to make sure there is no leak and that the cargo is intact."

"Surely. It is always a pleasure to serve you."

The boat was winched over the side with Judith and the crewman aboard and the ship's dinghy then pulled it to shore with them in it.

* * *

Ethel opened the door of her room and was faced with the hotel concierge, hand raised, about to knock.

"Oh, Signora, I came to tell you that your husband telephoned. He is coming here tomorrow. He asked me not to tell you because he wanted to surprise you, but I thought you would want to know so that you could prepare yourself properly. I would want to know that myself."

"Thank you," stammered Ethel, turning pale. "I was about to go shopping. What time does his ferry arrive?"

* * *

Just as elsewhere in southern Italy, the *passeggiata* is practiced on Stromboli in summer. After sundown, people leave their houses and stroll the streets, greeting one another and gossiping. It is not nearly as crowded as in the mainland cities. The usual route is along the seaside road, up to the church piazza, and back down again by another street. In recent months, the same young man Carl had followed into Barbablu the first day on the island had instituted a fire dance he learned in Tahiti in the church piazza some nights, assisted by others he had trained in this curious skill. They twirled and swung baton-like sticks burning at each end in the darkness, sometimes flinging them high into the air and catching them adroitly when they came down. They danced in a row while doing this, chanting a Polynesian song, while a row of drummers beat out a rhythm. It was spectacular for little Stromboli, and each set was loudly applauded by strollers who gathered in crowds to watch.

A short distance down the road from the church piazza, the Prime Numbers were having dinner at Barbablu, out under the grape arbor on the side of the building. They had arrived in a swarm of Apes taxis and entered through an outside gate, and now there were five tables of them, six men seated at each. Mark was standing and clinking a spoon on a glass to get their attention in order to propose a toast when the specially hired waitresses for this large dinner party entered with the wine and the antipasto course. A waitress with a carafe in each hand, one of red wine, the other of white, approached Mark's table and had placed them there when she glanced at Mark and her jaw dropped.

"Marco?" she asked loudly.

"Carmencita," he replied, even louder, standing and throwing up both hands.

They embraced emotionally, both laughing, Mark saying, "No, no," and Carmencita "Yes, yes," with tears in her eyes. The men at Mark's table watched with smiles and applause, unaware of exactly what was happening.

With an arm around her waist and a kiss to her cheek, Mark, who by now had the attention of all the tables, said loudly, "This is my little cousin Carmencita. We were children together in Pomigliano, a few miles north of Naples. Her mother and my mother are sisters, but after my parents and I, still a boy, moved to America, we lost touch."

There was another round of applause, wine glasses were filled, and the reunion was toasted with cheers. Mark got a chair for her to sit next to him but she shook her head.

"No, no, Marco, I cannot. I am working. After," she said and did the Neapolitan gesture for later, hand pointing over her shoulder, and left for the kitchen, looking back once and laughing.

"Isn't that the wildest thing," said Mark, shaking his head, wiping his eyes, and sitting down once more.

* * *

The Prime Number's dinner at Barbablu was about to break up when Carl realized that someone was standing beside his chair. The fat man leaned forward and spoke quietly into his ear.

"Carl, it is time."

"Please excuse me," Carl said to the table and walked with the fat man a short distance away.

"What do you mean?"

"Come. We must leave now."

"Uh, sir, leave?"

"Yes. Come."

Carl hesitated and then followed the fat man out of the arbor, through the door, and into the street.

"But ..." he had begun when a hand was placed on his shoulder, and he turned to find Patroclus grinning at him. He placed his hand on top of that of Patroclus, an unmistakable lover's touch.

"We are taking a boat," said the fat man.

"The three of us are going out in a boat now?"

"Yes. You may not refuse. Patroclus is coming only because of you."

"Ah, well, in that case, wonderful. I will just tell Mark ..."

"Come now. There is not time to tell Mark anything."

The boy put his arm around Carl's shoulder and looked into his eyes. Carl shrugged, and the three of them walked briskly to the next corner and then turned downhill on the steep cross street and headed for the beach.

Nobody at the dinner missed Carl.

* * *

Later, when dinner was over and the Prime Numbers were standing in a raucous group outside Barbablu waiting to board the golf cart-like Apes for the rides back to the hotel, two of them on one side of the group were talking.

"Hal, you are asking me about the meaning of life? Me, the village idiot faggot? Darling, it's Harry of Harry and George, remember?"

"Uh, Harry, I know that you do this camp pose, but I know too that it is the result of you having been hurt, probably when you were young. Underneath that, I don't see any fool at all. On the contrary, I have heard how well you have managed your life."

"Well, thank you for that, but maybe there is nothing here but the fool after all. I'm very flattered. What's your question?"

"If truth and honesty are so desirable, how is it that everyone lies incessantly? Why wasn't lying weeded out from society long, long ago?"

"I know the answer to that, and you must too. It's pragmatism, darling, simple pragmatism. If you can dupe fellow men into babbling by lying to them about the purity of such goals as honesty and openness, then you can locate and grab their assets more easily, feed your own progeny, have more children, and perpetuate the genetic basis for your cleverness. That what you want to hear?"

"It's all a scam? Law is a scam too?"

"No, love, law's purpose is to protect the holdings you have stolen from the drones."

"Then I would think that these drones in society all would have starved to death millenia ago."

"Sweetie, you fail to see that they function as a kind of serving class and are permitted to reproduce because of their very usefulness. They gather the assets that the smarter people will steal."

"That's pretty cynical, Harry."

"Hal, you were the man complaining about the universality of lying. Talk about cynicism. You already knew it was useful, you just needed me to tell you how. And by the way, pussy, turn down your collar. The sixties are over, you know."

"Got it, Harry. Listen, I'm not Sigmund Freud, but I would like to hear about your childhood."

"I was the apple of everyone's eye."

"No, really."

"It would upset you. Give you nightmares. Upset your ideas about wonderful family life with Jimmy Stewart."

"It might fill in some blanks instead."

"Okay, you want it? Here it is. When I was a tiny boy, my father once found me playing with myself, painted my crotch red with mercurochrome, and stood me naked before the whole family, who all whooped and pointed in derision. When I was older, he would take me on hunting trips with his buddies. They all got blind drunk in camp at night and he would make me literally piss up a tree while they stood around and guffawed at my discomfiture."

"Oops. Pretty awful, Harry. Where was this?"

"Texas, the nut state, where else? They still do it there."

"I think I read somewhere about painting little boys' genitals red, maybe it was Texas. You ever see any of these people now?"

"Well, they're mostly dead, but recently two of them showed up at my door in Palm Springs saying they were broke and looking for help. My personal assistant answered the door and let them in. I made sure that they got a good look around that mid-century showplace house and heard about some of my assets, and then I personally showed them out the door and told them to go piss up a tree. Revenge is sweet. It was nearly perfect closure. I have as little to do with straight society now as possible. They all are assholes."

"When did that happen?"

"Only last year. Before it happened, I wouldn't have been able to talk to you like this at all. Some of the bitterness and rage just evaporated afterward. Look, Hal, would you like to walk back to the hotel instead of riding? It is a lovely night."

* * *

Mark was one of many people on the island who woke much later in the night to the roisterous noises of what he thought must be a drunken party of very loud revelers moving through the village and away somewhere. Before going back to sleep, he hoped that the sounds did not involve any Prime Numbers. Many people in the village heard it too. Some looked outside to see who it was, but they didn't see anyone. In fact, it was the entire island population of very raucous ravens flying away en masse to the east in the dark of the moon, off the island, and disappearing out to sea.

The few boats of very late sightseers going out to view the crater display and the earliest fishing boats were marked by red or green lights as seen from the shore, according to the direction in which they headed: red if toward the crater slide area, green when returning. The light on the 190-foot-high summit of Strombolicchio flashed an unerring three quick white flashes every fifteen seconds from its twenty-six-foot-tall tower. The seismograph drum in the volcano museum loudly hummed a quickening universal harmony that no staff was on duty to applaud, nor would they be there the next day, a holiday.

An hour before dawn, there were three closely spaced reports like cannon shots that were heard all over the island. The islanders recognized them as explosions from the crater, not so unusual, and nobody was alarmed.

* * *

Probably, he thought, one sea anchor would have been adequate for stability of the strange little craft in which they floated, and Carl said this to the fat man.

"Yes, but two will give more stability, and besides, their function for us is to utilize the current for movement rather than to keep a bow into the wind."

And so, leaning over the gunwale in the light from the village on shore, Carl threw one tethered canvas bucket into the water as the fat man threw another one close by. There was a jerk that reminded Carl of a San Francisco cable car grasping a moving cable, and they were jolted forward surprisingly rapidly. The lights of the hotel and then the village were left astern in only a few minutes, and the glow of the crater appeared from around an occlusion point.

"Seems like an unusually strong current."

"Yes and it will become stronger."

"Are we doing this right?"

"Yes."

Judith and Patroclus sat silently on the padded bench surrounding the interior perimeter of the strange, round little craft. The sea gurgled beneath the fiberglass hull. With an effort, the fat man pulled a hinged sectional dome into place above them, and Judith lit a candle in a glass container. They were completely enclosed within a boat of circular outline with a dome covering.

"It's like a little temple," remarked Carl.

"Indeed," responded the fat man.

"We are not going out to see the crater display after all, are we?"

"No. I never said that."

"Where are we going?"

"Cap Bon."

"Where is Cap Bon?"

"Tunisia."

Carl looked at him with widened eyes. "But …" he began.

"I know, Carl," said the fat man. "It will all become clear to you soon. Meanwhile, emulate Patroclus. He is unconcerned."

At this, Patroclus smiled a wonderfully contented smile at Carl and shrugged his shoulders.

The fat man closed his eyes and leaned back against a pile of loose cushions while Judith lighted two more candles. The interior became quite bright.

"Should I say something?" asked Carl.

"If you wish," said the fat man.

"We are going to Tunisia. It is a surprise to me. I have not said good-bye to my friends. May I ask for an explanation? For example, why in this odd boat?"

"The ashes and cinders would clog any engine. There will be no winds for a sail. The dome will prevent us and the hull from being harmed by falling rocks and keep the boat from filling and sinking. The circular shape will lessen damage to any one part of the hull from floating pumice blocks."

"You are describing a volcanic eruption. Is it to be Stromboli?"

"Correct. Stromboli."

"When?"

"Enough for the moment, please. You are handling your destiny well. Patroclus will sing for us now. He knows the old songs. They are soothing. Try to sleep."

Outside and unseen, the brightly glowing crater passed off their larboard, the boat moved on into the darkness, and Patroclus began a first song. He sang of Odysseus leaving Aeolus with the bag of winds. He sang in the language of Homer. Carl slept.

X. FLAMEOUT

The sun rose on Stromboli for the last time. Harry, awake early and watching it from the hotel room balcony, extended a straight arm and measured its place on the horizon as exactly three fists to the right of Strombolicchio. The dawn was clear and cloudless and changed colors as he watched from gray to orange to pink to blue, so pretty that he almost waked George and Frederick to see but thought better of it when he noticed how contentedly they were wrapped around one another in bed. Three beach dogs crossed the black sand together and waded into the sea for a cooling swim, paddling about and yapping delightedly at one another. Anchored off the beach were seven sloops and one ketch with furled sails, one yacht, and four motor boats, all with bows pointed eastward, tugging on their anchor lines in the windless morning. The *Stella di Lipari* had chugged away on schedule an hour before dawn. A sudden light wind swung all the boats and caused an occlusion of the hulls of the sloops and ketch so that momentarily they appeared to Harry to be one boat with four masts. As the church bell in the village pealed for early mass, the smell of coffee came up to him from the restaurant below. He rose and went indoors to shower and dress for breakfast.

After pulling on a funk Dolce and Gabbana t-shirt and a pair of baggy shorts, Harry sat down on his bed to buckle on his sandals. As he bent over, he was nearly face-to-face with sleeping Frederick in the next bed. Frederick opened one eye.

"Morning."

"Oh, hello, Fred. You're awake."

"We've been awake for some time. We're working."

"You're working?"

"Yes, we're writing a song. When our heads touch like this, we can hum lightly and set the melody. We pass it back and forth. Almost finished now."

"What about words?"

George didn't move but said quietly. "Almost finished too. We may call it 'Highway One-Eleven.'"

"Hasn't something like that been used?"

"Nothing like this has ever been done. Go to breakfast, and we will finish it and sing it for you when you come back."

Fred closed his eyes again, and they literally put their heads together. Harry walked out of the room into the hall, clicking the room door shut behind him, and headed for the restaurant downstairs, wondering if he should speak to George and Frederick about the stuff they had bought from that louche fellow at the beach yesterday.

The song name already had been changed to "Click."

* * *

Is prettiness a spoiler? Of course, it can be, leading to crass clichés, even to grotesqueries such as the American country club look with couples not only overly prettified themselves but even with each spouse looking like an interchangeable drag version of the other. And yet, a simple or simplified prettiness has universal appeal. It was the latter kind that both William and Marutus worked to create professionally where it was called for. An artistic director and an event designer have many attributes in common.

The Sorrentine peninsula too has been overworked in part by people with only prettiness in mind, and some places even today are cloying in the extreme with pretty frames for views, pretty decorations, prettily clad attendants, and even pretty names, many dating from nineteenth-century Romanticism. Kitsch. And yet the integrity of such a place can rise above these human artifacts and effortlessly recapture the real spirit of prettiness.

The Pathway of the Gods is the kitsch name of a quite lovely hiking trail that connects villages in the Lattari Mountains of the Sorrentine peninsula. Marutus and William were walking along it after a drive uphill from Ravello to a trail head. There would be a stop for lunch at a village restaurant in about an hour, and then they would return the same way. Everywhere there were wild flowers, trees, wild herbs, rocks, views, odors, birds, scurrying animals, the blowing wind, and sundry sounds. It was very pretty indeed in the best sense.

"Will," Marutus was saying, "you know that I am crazy about you. I would like us to live the good life together, lovers and partners. Forever. What do you say?"

"Yes, I would be happy with that myself. Of course, you are tied here to the opera, while I could work anywhere. So it would mean me moving, relocating my business, and all that implies, but I do think that we were meant to be together."

"My thoughts too. Then, is it agreed and we now can work on details?"

"Yes, it is agreed. Give me your hand on the contract. I do not need an emotional explosion, but I would sign in blood if you wanted it."

And so they grasped hands firmly, kissed lightly, and continued their walk, arm-in-arm, bodies touching, almost fraternally. Very pretty indeed. Very sincere.

"You know, William," said Marutus a little later, "I immediately was attracted to you, and there have been many small things that have pleased me immensely. Want to hear one of the most endearing?"

"Ummm."

"Your quietness. The lack of the inane, mindless chatter that most gay men engage in. Especially early morning. You have never asked that stupid question about how well I slept."

"Then you surely will like my friends David and Carolyn. The first night I stayed with them, Carolyn told me before we went to bed that in the morning there would be coffee and muffins and a New York Times for each of us in the kitchen but that they did not want any conversation before noon."

"Very civilized. I like them already. Do they travel? We must have them here."

"I already had planned on asking them."

"Very good," said Marutus, "I wonder how your other friends are enjoying Stromboli."

* * *

The ferry from Palermo arrived at Stromboli, announced moments before it bumped the busy pier by two blasts from its horn. The first off was a young Sicilian priest in robe and collar, accompanied by a dozen teenaged men, each of whom carried a pasteboard box that he put on the pier and then returned to the boat for more, until there was a head-high stack of them built up. Hank, waiting on one side of the exit door while they unloaded their cargo, thought of Mexico, where priests were forbidden to wear robes and collars in public, and of America, where recent scandals probably would preclude the propriety of such a group in public. When they had taken the last box ashore, he walked down the gangplank to the pier and into the waiting crowd to find directions to Ethel's hotel.

* * *

Ethel was seated at an early lunch in the garden restaurant of her hotel, expecting Hank to arrive sometime that day, and bravely prepared to have it out with him and simply send him away. She had gathered her wits, taken a tranquilizer, and gone to see the village police, one of whom had listened distractedly to her story and then informed her that the police were uninterested in domestic squabbles but that someone would come if the husband became physically abusive. He gave her his telephone number. The waiter came to her table with dishes on a tray.

"Say, did you hear something?" she said to the him moments before they both were vaporized by the first descending glowing avalanche.

Next came a major explosion from the crater, triggered by magmatic gases that were forced up from deep in the chamber as molten rock rose from below. The top of Stromboli was completely blown off, and a Plinian cloud of ash and rock pushed up into the stratosphere. Giant blocks tumbled wildly down all slopes of the volcano, including through the villages and into the sea. They were followed by wide, anastamosing, rapidly moving streams of basalt giving the island briefly a fudge sundae look until the ash began to fall and blocked out the sun.

As more magma was pumped up from below, expansion cracks opened in the neck and on the submarine slopes of the volcano, admitting enormous quantities of sea water, preparing the way for the steam explosions that would destroy the entire island within hours.

A pumice fall covered the surrounding sea almost at once and trailed off twenty miles to the east. Great blocks of this floating rock ground noisily against one another in the violent and erratic waves as tsunamis swept up the shores and then withdrew to below normal sea level.

Lightning flashes rent all the ash falls, and thunder rivaled the volcanic explosions for Wagnerian effect.

The lighthouse inspector who was at work on Strombolicchio was one of the few people to live more than a few minutes following the beginning of the eruption. He understood what was happening and watched in horror from the tower as the great blasts erupted into the sky with unbelievable force and noise and the glowing clouds and lava flows poured down the slopes.

When the lava chamber below had emptied enough for caldera formation to be imminent, the block bearing Strombolicchio, its lighthouse, and the keeper was the first to crack and then be transported straight down into an underworld so fabulous that no mythological place could do it justice. He rode his lighthouse down, free fall at first, through a waterfall of ocean water two miles tall to a crash landing on an incredibly hot, even partially molten, rock floor. Next, the lighthouse and keeper, now dead, and much of Strombolicchio were hurled straight up again, out of the chamber and high into the black sky above the churning sea by the phreatic explosion as the sea water reached the molten magma on the chamber floor, flashed to steam, and expanded mightily. Finally there was another two-mile fall to the surface of the sea for the keeper's body and a slow sink to the sea bottom, where he sleeps today with the fishes.

At the end, much later, there was nothing left of Stromboli at sea level but an incomplete ring marking the outer extremities of the volcano, very little of which extended above the sea. Almost immediately, the lava plug in the center of the ring was forced upward by the residual pressure in fits. It crumbled under the sea and rose upward again and again so that eventually it broke the surface of the sea as a resurgent lava dome, a tiny island marking the center of the once great Stromboli, Lighthouse of the Mediterranean, now extinguished forever.

* * *

The sonic boom from the Stromboli eruption hit Naples a few minutes after intromission. The building shuddered once and eardrums popped throughout almost the whole of southern Italy. Bones swallowed to clear his ears but didn't miss a stroke, working it the way that first had made his name in San Francisco, an Olympian fuck, a laurel wreath fuck, brutal, deliberate, exquisite.

Again and again the body beneath him arched the small of its back to the limit imposed by the vertebrae and then pressed it flat against the floor. The first ground wave from Stromboli rocked the building, accompanied by a long, deep howl that rose from the earth and cracks and snaps from the grinding joists of the twisting building.

"Oh, god."

"He won't help you this time. It's my show now."

Plaster dust fell lightly from the ceiling until it had coated both sweaty bodies, including even the red hair, turning them into a tableau of Greek wrestler statues in action, worthy of Praxiteles, working with the greatest restraint through the greatest passion, with the greatest deliberation through the greatest abandon. The sun passed its nadir and still Bones pounded, sweat pouring in rivulets from the hair in his armpits. The bottom spoke again, a guttural whisper.

"Choke me a little."

"In a minute. I call the shots here."

And in exactly a minute, he did, and wild spurting shots from both were called, and then after the dripping body beneath him had collapsed, he stayed pushed in to full hilt and kept the pressures on the two neck arteries too until the throbs there ceased at last and only the tiny pulses in his own two thumbs still beat.

There was a great sigh, a gargle, and the eyes opened wide for a brief second in recognition and wonderment before they glazed over forever.

Bones withdrew slowly, rose to his feet, showered, carefully shaved, dressed, left the hillside building, and just directed his feet to the sunny side of the street, where crowds had gathered to watch the distant black and gray Plinian cloud spreading into the stratosphere, soon to dim the sunlight even in Naples.

He recognized a neighbor in the crowd and asked, "Where is it?"

"They say Stromboli."

* * *

"Dadd-ee!" shrieked little Helen from the garden, where she was teasing a cat with a piece of paper tied to a string. "Dadd-ee, what is that in the sky?"

John put his work down and left the piano for the patio. Indeed, there on the horizon was a great mushroom cloud.

"Is it a volcano?" asked Helen in a quieter voice.

"No, dearest," said Mary, who had come from the house and stood beside John. "The volcano is over there, see? Vesuvius looks normal."

"It looks like pictures of an atom bomb explosion," John remarked.

"But, dear," said Mary, "there is nothing out there but ocean and then Sicily. Who would want to blow up Sicily?"

"Let's turn on TV," suggested Helen.

The news indeed indicated a catastrophe of some kind, with officials speaking into the camera interspersed with confusing scenes of people pouring off a ferry.

"It's all in Italian. I can't understand a thing," said John.

"He says it's an island and that everyone is dead," piped up Helen.

"Darling, you have learned Italian after all," cooed Mary, patting Helen on the head.

"What do you think we speak in school all day long?"

* * *

William and Marutus had finished lunch on the back terrace at the Villa Cimbrone and were talking at table about various Prime Numbers. Only one other table was occupied.

"So, that's a thumbnail about Carl," said Marutus. "You know that our director at the opera is interested in him. I think that he will pursue it, at least a little."

"Carl is attractive and also trustworthy, that most important quality. I wish your director success."

"Something that puzzles him, though, is that Carl has been seen around the opera house with one of our local characters, a very fat one. Do you know anything about that?"

"No, but Carl is quite independent. And he's apparently single. Why the interest in his friends?"

"The man is strange. It would be nice to know their relationship."

"What do you mean?"

"When he was young, the fat man was a dancer with the opera ballet, and his sister was a singer with the chorus. Then something happened, I am told, and they both got a reputation for unacceptable absenteeism. They were dismissed, but they continued to be friends with some of the opera employees. The dancer put on a lot of weight fast and was thought to be mentally unbalanced. The director suspects that he was that odalisque who commandeered *Aida* the other night. He has been told that they sometimes actually live somewhere in the opera house. It is a warren of rooms in the basements and attics. For example, the once-secret passages to the next door royal palace are famous and still exist. They easily could live undetected in the building."

"Well, Marutus, I don't know Carl well enough to be privy to his intimate life. But, I will ask if you wish."

"Yes, please. I wish. No harm would come from giving me this information."

The waitress came with a bill to be signed, said "Signores," and pointed to a towering cloud on the horizon of the sea.

"What is it?" asked William.

"She says an eruption."

"Etna?"

"Apparently Stromboli."

"Oh, babe, no."

* * *

Carl was wakened by a drumming on the roof, like hail. He sat up and saw that the others in their little boat already were awake. There were new candles, and the cabin seemed warm and comfortable, even cozy, a refuge. The noise increased, then faded somewhat, then increased again to a roar that was punctuated by erratically spaced loud bangs when larger stones fell from the sky. This became the background, like drums, together with the fainter gray noise of floating pumice grinding against the hull, over which they had to speak for the next several hours.

Patroclus handed him a basket of figs and dates, and Judith poured him a cup of herbal tea. The fat man, Judith, and Patroclus already were eating and drinking. Carl removed a handful of dates and several figs and put them alongside himself on the bench. He tried the tea and nodded in approval. They soon all were eating and laughing, a party atmosphere.

"Carl," said the fat man, "there are rituals to be gone through, the mysteries. Because of the special circumstances of our present state and because of your maturity, I will greatly simplify them. Believe me that they have been elaborate indeed in many previous ceremonies, right Judith?"

Judith smiled and nodded.

"I am prepared," Carl replied, "to believe almost anything at this point. The falling scoriae must be the collapsing Plinian cloud from a Stromboli eruption, yes? I can believe that. What I do not know is how you knew in advance."

"Patience, that will be revealed. Yes, Stromboli blew and is gone. Almost nothing remains of that once substantial island. It will be many thousand years before it rebuilds."

Carl did not look disturbed but said, "I could see from the geologic maps that there had been previous islands in the same geographic position of Stromboli, and I could imagine future similar ones. The existence of Strombolicchio was further evidence. And everyone there must have died in this eruption if Stromboli no longer exists, correct?"

"Yes, unhappily for them. I am sorry."

"Now can we proceed with your mysteries? How do we begin?"

"Carl, I am the Lord Bacchus, and you are my apostle."

"I accept your statement, and I had assumed something of the kind."

"And," the fat man continued, "I will grant you certain favors that will simplify your future work greatly."

"Please do so."

"I grant you and Patroclus the language gift."

"Hello," said Patroclus, almost shyly.

"I grant you, Carl, limited foreknowledge."

"That works. Things are clearer to me now."

"I grant you both long life."

"And youth?" asked Patroclus. "Please youth too. We don't want to make the Sibyl's mistake."

"Carl, see how helpful Patroclus will be to you? And his youth to Patroclus and his present age to Carl.

"And I grant you both full knowledge of the Mysteries."

"Oh," expostulated Carl. "A little difficult to handle that. Is it all accurate?"

"It is. You will spread hope and joy through celebration. Wherever you go, the work continues. It is Patroclus' duty to assist you in whatever capacity you wish, including that of lover. He will be more than adequate in everything and even will improve over time."

"And I sense, sir, that you and I will travel separately."

"Yes, but occasionally our paths will cross. Judith will see you and Patroclus even more often."

"A lot to grasp in such a brief time. And the drumming on the roof has stopped. What does it mean?"

"We have moved from beneath the collapsing cloud. The mystery ceremony is completed. Landfall will be soon. Have some more tea. It will help take the edge off."

"Sir, may I say that I was taught that revelations are signs of madness or illness such as epilepsy or induced by gases and drugs or otherwise are fictions and deliberate frauds. Something nobody could verify."

"Carl, there is another way. You have just experienced it."

"Then the Revelation of John might have been valid?"

"Carl, you are excited. This is not the time for that discussion. Please wait. It will come. I know you have patience."

"I see. Yes, I can wait. There are so many questions I want answered about what you have given to me. Sir, you said there is another way. 'It will come to you,' you said. You are an amazing man, sir."

"So it has been said."

Suddenly, Carl laughed. He guffawed with abandon, clutching his sides. They all laughed. The little craft shook with their laughter. The laughing sister nodded to the laughing brother with approval. Patroclus laughed most of all.

* * *

"Kill the fatted calf, Mary. It is done."

Mary smiled and wiped her hands before leaving the sink and embracing John.

"Oh, John," she said, "I'm so glad. A thousand congratulations. And now we can catch our scheduled flight home on Friday."

"Yes, I'm glad too. I will fax the whole package to New York today. What a relief."

"Yes," came a young voice from the living room. "What a relief. I am so sick of Naples that I could scream."

The laughter that followed was genuine too.

* * *

"There, Patroclus," directed the fat man. "Unfasten that latch. We can collapse the dome. Our craft has done its duty well, but that need is now past."

They carefully lowered each hinged section into the groove along the boat's perimeter. Sunlight flooded in, and a seascape with a great, barren, rocky headland of a pale orange hue appeared, surprisingly nearby. The sun shone through the gray clouds in angled shafts, illuminating the choppy, still troubled sea, heaving and lowering in the near shore areas before breaking noisily against the cliffs and rushing up and withdrawing from the cobbled beaches. Large rafts of gray pumice floated in the sea, but they were breaking up. A humid north wind blew over the sea, smelling now of late summer flowers in Sicily.

"That's Cap Bon, Carl," said the fat man. "Tunisia. We will land there, and someone from the nearby village will come to meet us."

It was slow progress to the shore, but at last their boat was in a narrow cove surrounded by a flat, rocky shelf. Patroclus took the end of the line the fat man handed him, waited until the boat rose in the swell to the proper height, and leapt ashore. He pulled the boat to the inner reaches of the cove where the surge was almost absent and helped Judith and the fat man out onto the marine terrace near the white ruins of a one room, ancient building, still wet, with a pumice-strewn floor from the last of the tsunamis. Carl handed Patroclus cloth bags filled with belongings as directed by the fat man and then, when there were no further directions, asked a question.

"And what else?"

There was nothing else. Carl jumped from the boat to the rocky shelf. The fat man took the line from Patroclus and threw it into the boat, which floated away and out into the sea.

"Someone will find it and be delighted," he said. "They use everything here. Please sit."

They all sat down on the rock. The fat man opened one of the canvas bags and handed a package to Carl.

"Here are passports, cash, and credit cards with which you may pay bills and withdraw money at any ATM machine. You two will go to Tangier for starters. Something is building there.

Judith and I are going to Alexandria for the long-delayed opening of Alexander's tomb."

"They located it at last?" asked Carl.

"Yes, still sealed. The entrance simply buried beneath the mosque. Octavian in the end was very thoughtful. He not only replaced Alexander's breastplate on the great man's body from which Cleopatra had removed it as a gift to Antony, he also transferred the bodies of the famous lovers to Alexander's tomb before he re-sealed it and covered the entrance. The event will be spectacular. She still is dressed as the Living Isis, and he in the blood-encrusted general's regalia he wore when he botched his suicide, with the sword nearby. Alexander is in his rock crystal sarcophagus, his broken nose alongside his face where she left it after Antony touched it and broke it off. You will see details on the news."

"But here we are, meanwhile, on this rocky point," commented Carl.

Patroclus pointed to a distant dust plume, which turned out to be a jeep headed for them. They soon were on their ways, first to the nearby fishing village of El Haouaria and then to the world.

* * *

And friends, if there be angels—a pretty but wholly illogical concept—they could now come forward to chant a clear song of remembrance in praise of our acquaintances lost on Stromboli, perhaps a countertenor or even castrati mode would be appropriate here, whatever the dead might deem pleasing if they still were quick. Who knows? Do I not hear something? Do you? Listen.

XI. OLD WINE INTO NEW BOTTLES

Mary woke instantly to a sudden, shrill scream in the night from outside the house. She sat up, turned on the bedside lamp, saw that John was asleep still, and shook him.

"John, wake up. Something is wrong outside. I'm going to look."

He groggily swung his legs over the side of the bed as she rushed out the bedroom door, pulling on a robe. In the living room, she saw that the house door was open, turned on the patio lights, went out, and was met by little Helen running barefoot up from the garden.

"Mother, I was bitten by a spider."

John came to the door and shone his flashlight onto a disappearing Vespa that sped up the dark driveway, past the landlord's house, and toward the street above.

"What do you mean you were bitten by a spider? What are you doing out here at this time of night? What's going on?"

A light went on in the house higher on the property, and they saw the landlord lean out a window, then disappear again. A moment later, their phone rang, and John went to answer it.

"Yes, everything is all right. Just some family excitement, nothing to worry about. Thank you for calling," he said to the landlord.

He returned to the patio to find Mary saying testily to Helen, "It was Diana's brother, wasn't it? You don't have to tell me. Now come inside this instant."

As they went in the front door, John noticed a bright red footprint where they had been standing and shone his flashlight on it.

"What's this blood?" he asked loudly.

"John," said Mary, "Helen and I are going into the bathroom. Everything will be under control in a few minutes."

"No," he stammered incredulously. "She's only ten years old."

"Actually, she's eleven, going on twelve, and there is something we haven't told you."

"You don't mean … ?"

"Yes, everything happens earlier these days. Go make some coffee, and I will come in after Helen goes to bed."

Even as Mary and Helen walked into the bathroom and John to the kitchen, the wall of an egg harbored by young Helen was breached by a vigorous sperm, which dropped its tail, moved inside the cell, taking with it some old Roman genes that descended in direct line from the Emperor Nero's genetic makeup and furiously combined with recessive genes in Helen's egg. John and Mary all too soon would have a most interesting grandson indeed, in the sense of the old Neapolitan curse, "May your life be interesting." The boy and his mother would give new depth to their concepts of perfidy. But that's another story.

FINIS

POSTSCRIPTUM

For readers who may wish to know what life was like for the characters who lived on, I provide the following:

FRANK BONES. Bones lived in Naples another thirty years, walking almost daily to his office at the university geology department, where he used the collections and library to pen and publish more than two hundred scientific papers that made the restored, again hallowed Kingdom of Two Sicilies (Empress Maria Carolina II became his patroness) one of the best-known fossil floral areas of the world. On his death, his was the second body lain anonymously in the crypt beneath his condo building, which then was sealed, never to be reopened.

JOHN CAMPBELL. John had a successful Broadway career and remained married to Mary until his death. The day he was diagnosed with early Alzheimer's disease, their daughter Helen had him institutionalized. John and Mary died within days of one another in a Boston hospital.

SISTER JANE. Jane quickly found another "brother," the purser of the tour ship on which she and Hank had met Ethel. They resumed the same scam and eventually retired, very wealthy, to London, a large house in Kensington, where they died after long residence. Interpol never showed the slightest interest in them.

WILLIAM WESTON and MARUTUS TAYLOR. Marutus and William became iconic lovers in international society. They were noted as superb hosts, with accommodations at the Palazzo Donn'Anna and also a villa on the cliffs at Ravello, which they bought from a famous gay writer. They lived to very old ages and died within a year of one another.

JUDITH. She remains with her brother, a devoted colleague and companion.

CARL CRAVEN. Dear Carl moves even today about the world with the beautiful Patroclus, turning heads everywhere they go. They perform their duties with flying colors and are successful lovers too in all the best senses. Naples is a special city for them, and they return often, where they have become close friends with the director of the San Carlo Opera.

THE LORD BACCHUS. The fat man will continue to lighten the load for humanity for a very long time, the exact length of which I am not at liberty to disclose.

Acknowledgments

There are so many people I wish to thank for so very many kindnesses given me during the preparation of this book that I will list only names for the sake of brevity and hope that they will forgive me for any perceived slight because of the lack of detail. I am grateful to each and every one of you and in your debts forever: Jan Adlmann, Angelo Di Maio, Diana Fattori, William Fletcher, Suzanne Goell, Michael Craft Johnson, Hussein Elkhakim, Willie Lebron, Nando Musmarra, Lionel Nason, Gustl and Valerie Schuldes, Giovanni Batista Solferino and Ronald Taylor. I especially wish to thank Dr. Lorenza Mochi Onori for permission to use the painting by Andy Warhol titled "Vesuvius" that hangs in the Capodimonte Museum in Naples.